A Destiny Reborn

Prevent the Past, Book 2

By Rebecca Hefner

Cover Design: Anthony O'Brien, www.BookCoverDesign.store
Editor: Megan McKeever
Sensitivity Reader: Harper Miller, www.authorharpermiller.com
Proofreader: Bryony Leah, www.bryonyleah.com

*Because I fell in love with Cyrus and Claire in A Paradox of Fates and had
to write their love story...*

Table of Contents

Chapter 1

September 2, 2075

Claire Finch stood in the underground bunker, eyes wide as she observed Lainey and Hunter clutch hands inside the Sphere. The massive contraption's arms were whirling violently, creating a vortex that would upend the rules of time and space. Although she wore a protective suit to shield her from the radiation she would encounter when she traveled next, Claire hadn't yet donned the plastic hood. Holding it against her hip, her free hand shook with awe and fear as Lainey gave the nod to Zach to ignite the fuel rod. It would give them the boost needed to travel back in time, where they would focus all their efforts on preventing the apocalypse and saving the world.

In this dystopian timeline, Lainey's grandfather, President Edward James Randolph, had detonated America's nuclear arsenal in 2035, plunging the world into chaos. An evil regime called the New Establishment had toiled for decades to control every corner of the post-apocalyptic planet, and they were now on the cusp of world domination. Only by traveling to 2035 and preventing the past could a new timeline emerge, along with the hope of a brighter future.

A warmth enveloped Claire's hand, strong and sure, as anxiety laced her veins. After all, Lainey was her best friend, her confidant, and a mother figure of sorts. Claire loved her dearly. If something happened to her, she would be devastated. The man beside Claire understood this, and that comforted her, for Cyrus had somehow become her rock. Smiling up at him, she compressed his hand, silently thanking him for his thoughtful reassurance.

Her feelings for him were complex and simple, both at once. She didn't know when or how she'd fallen down the chasm of love with the strong, stoic soldier, but it had happened all the same. Although she understood he didn't return her romantic feelings, that didn't seem to matter to her heart, which he now possessed even though she was certain he had no idea she was secretly enamored. Claire equated it to the natural rock formation she'd adored as a child, all those years ago, on the outskirts of Solera. It jutted from the river, looming and hardened. Slick with summer rain, she would sit at the top and stare down, sure that if she glided down the slippery surface she'd drown at the bottom. But even as a child, she was brave—and a bit precocious—and had slithered down the wet stone, surging headlong into fear. Every time she landed, the water was warm and enveloping, reminding her there was reward at the end of risk.

Glancing up at Cyrus, Claire reveled in his calloused skin against her comparative softness. Just as she'd slid down the stone in her youth, she'd fallen so deeply into the abyss with him that a return to simple friendship was unlikely—on her end at least. The indomitable man beside her was tough to read. There were times when she glimpsed emotion in his deep brown eyes, but she was never sure of the true sentiment. Did he see her as just another asset to protect? Someone he cared for and had a sworn duty toward? Or did he truly *see* her—Claire covered in layers of dyed hair and multicolored fingernails to hide her other flaws? Claire with the bubbly personality she exhibited not only because it was her true nature, but because it was easier to live that way than admit she lived in a world where she didn't belong; a soldier in a war she'd enlisted in due to other people's decisions, and one she was so tired of fighting?

It probably seemed overly simplistic to those as dedicated to saving humanity as Lainey and Cyrus: the idea of living a normal life, raising a family, and not having to constantly worry about preventing an apocalypse, solving time travel, or saving the world. Perhaps it was selfish. After all, Claire had a brilliant mind and had always used it to further the cause. But, unlike Lainey, the cause didn't drive her; didn't push her to wake up each day and forge ahead. No, her motivating forces were much simpler.

Settling down. Living a simple life. Creating a family. Finding a husband who would challenge and love her even through dark and ominous times. Lacing her fingers through Cyrus's, she beamed at him, realizing she wanted those things with him. Wanted him to envelop her in his embrace and kiss away any lingering doubts and fears after a long day. And she desperately desired to return the sentiment. The familiar flashes of her daydreams took hold and she pushed them aside. Refocusing on the mission, she concentrated on the Sphere.

The wormhole opened behind Lainey and Hunter, portentous and devoid of light. It dragged Claire from her musings and filled her with a sense of foreboding. What if they perished? What if they failed? The possibilities were endless, and the unknowns were maddening to Claire's scientific brain.

Suddenly, Lainey and Hunter were sucked into the wormhole, and the bunker shook. Behind her, Zach clicked a menagerie of buttons, commencing the stabilization mode. The wormhole disappeared, and she looked at the kind, wiry scientist with the mop of dirty-blond hair behind the console.

"Time of transport of Dr. Elaine Randolph and Captain Hunter Rhodes to March 26, 2035 confirmed at twelve thirteen a.m. on September 2, 2075," Claire said.

"Confirmed," Zach replied, his tone heavy with the gravity of their actions.

Nodding, Claire released Cyrus's hand and turned to the group. "Cyrus and I are next. After that, Sara and Elle will follow, then Marie and Alora, then Zach. Ivan and Steven will then shut down and destroy the Sphere. I speak for all of us when I say 'thank you' to both of you. Your courage in staying behind is extremely noble. We all wish you a long and healthy life with your families in this timeline."

Ivan and Steven nodded, the loyal soldiers dedicated to the future they'd chosen. Claire thought it so brave. There was something so magnanimous about staying in a timeline where evil was certain to prevail in order to be with the ones you loved. She hoped if she was faced with a choice of that magnitude one day, she'd make the same decision.

The swirling arms of the Sphere came to a halt, and Cyrus placed an encouraging hand on her lower back. Elation that he was paired with her on their trip through time coursed through her. She'd always felt so safe with him. He led her up the stairs, quiet and pensive as usual, and they turned to face Zach. Donning their plastic hoods, they zipped them, ensuring they were protected from head to toe. Claire tilted her head at Zach, and he depressed the console button, causing the metal arms to clatter before beginning to twirl. For some reason, the sound startled her, and Cyrus grasped her hand, reminding her of his strength and fortitude. With him by her side, nothing could truly harm her. It was a belief as solid to her as the endless equations she'd solved with Lainey and Zach. Cyrus was unwavering and steady.

Thank god, because she was a quaking mess of nerves and fear.

The Sphere's arms reached maximum capacity, allowing for the bending of time and space. Giving a thumbs-up with her free hand, she saw Zach manipulate several buttons on the console and felt a tug behind her back. Flipping open the plastic cover, Zach lowered his hand to give the nuclear jolt needed to send them to 2035.

Suddenly, out of the corner of her eye, Claire saw the bright light. It blazed into the dim cavern from the opening above—the one that was supposed to be impenetrable to outsiders. A man climbed down the ladder, and she recognized him instantly: Eli Hernandez. Several soldiers dropped in behind him, all of them holding rifles.

Eli was the nefarious leader of the New Establishment on the Eastern Isle and perhaps the most feared man on the planet. Only days ago, Claire and Cyrus had learned he was actually a spy, visited by Lainey when he was only seven years old and groomed by her to infiltrate the New Establishment by way of his father, Victor. Whereas Eli was now a member of their team, albeit a secret member, Victor was the original driving force of the New Establishment. He'd worked with President Randolph to detonate the nukes and spent several decades systematically spreading the regime's malicious agenda.

Due to the whirling of the Sphere, Claire couldn't hear their conversation, but they seemed to be commanding Zach to shut down the time machine. Eli lifted a handgun from his belt and aimed it at her dear friend. Zach's eyes latched onto Claire's, and she saw the determination in them. Alora reached for her gun, still holstered at her waist. The woman was a fierce warrior and cunning as hell. Claire liked her chances against the men now holding them hostage. Claire focused her gaze on Zach, who gave her a final nod, and depressed the button that released the fuel rod jolt.

Claire was sucked into the wormhole, unsure if Cyrus had also been pulled in. Heavy, sticky forces of intense gravity choked her, and she struggled to open her eyes. Fisting her hands, she tried to draw into herself, to curl up and protect her body, but it was no use. She'd lost all control and was flying through the wormhole unencumbered by comfortable constants such as reality and normalcy. Bracing herself for what was to come, she gritted her teeth and strived to remain calm. Difficult, since her heart was pounding furiously inside her constricted chest. Struggling to breathe, she mentally commanded the nausea churning in her stomach to abate.

Finally, after an eternity of floating and spinning, she was met with a wall of grass and dirt. It thumped into her body, knocking the air from her lungs, and she gulped in a huge breath. Frantically searching for the zipper, she slid it open and pulled the plastic cover from her head. Palming the ground, she dry heaved, thankful she'd forgone dinner in an attempt to ward off an embarrassing barf session after the journey. As she gagged, her fingers dug into the ground, craving the stability of something still and unmoving. After several calming breaths, she gathered her wits.

Glancing behind her, she saw Cyrus. His large frame was still upon the grass, and her heart leaped into her throat. Crawling over, she unfastened his hood and removed it. Lowering her ear to his mouth, she listened for signs of life. It was faint, but he was breathing. Wanting to bring him to consciousness, she began lightly tapping his face. When that didn't work, she proceeded to hit him harder as concern mounted.

"Cyrus?" she yelled, slapping his cheek. "Wake up! Come on! You can do it."

Like a rabid snake, his hand dashed through the air, fingers encircling her wrist. Confused eyes snapped open, and his mahogany irises searched hers, dazed and disoriented.

"You're okay," she said, trying to sound calm over the pounding of her heart. "It's just me, Cyrus. We made it. We're intact, although you're squeezing the shit out of my arm."

His fingers released her immediately, contrition entering his gaze. "Claire?"

Chuckling, she nodded. "Yes, old man. It's me. I know you're almost senile, but you've got a few good years left. It's probable you hit your head and have a concussion. We came in for a pretty hard landing there."

His gaze darted over their surroundings. "Let me sit up," he said, gently pushing her away so he could take everything in. "Are we in 2035?"

Rotating to sit on the grass, she observed the forest they'd landed in. It was the spot Lainey had predetermined when she'd meticulously calculated the equations that would send them back to the past. The clearing was located far from prying eyes and was about a mile's walk from the warehouse where they would connect with Luke.

Luke was the first member of their team sent to the past, and their mission was to find him, Lainey, and Hunter once they'd landed.

As she surveyed the woods, Claire struggled to piece together what she'd observed before they transported.

"Did you see Eli and his soldiers enter the bunker?" she asked. "They appeared to be seizing the Sphere, but why? I thought Eli was on our side."

"I advised against trusting him," Cyrus said, "but Lainey was swayed. She has good instincts about these things. It's possible his deception was discovered by the New Establishment and he raided us to maintain the appearance of fighting against us."

"Speaking of Lainey, where are she and Hunter?"

Cyrus continued to survey the forest, eyes narrowed. "I don't know."

"They should be here," she said, pushing herself to stand and examining the sky through the thick trees. Wanting to be rid of the bulky suit, she divested it and grabbed her pack. After digging inside, she found the compass. Examining it, she faced west. "The sun is low to the horizon. I'd postulate it's about four thirty in the afternoon. We can wait for the others, but it's possible Eli will prevent anyone else from transporting. If they don't show, we need to walk to the warehouse before it gets dark."

Cyrus exhaled. "Okay. That's going to be tough though."

"Why?" Pivoting, she approached him.

As she neared, he shimmied out of the protective suit while still seated on the ground. Free of the orange material, he untied the laces of his black army boot and pulled it off, followed by the black sock. Pulling up the leg of his camouflage pants, he bared his ankle to her.

"Because of this."

Sucking in a breath, Claire stared down at the most swollen, discolored ankle she'd ever seen in her twenty-nine years on the planet.

Chapter 2

Cyrus's jaw clenched as he stared down at the mangled mess that was his left ankle. It throbbed, but he'd felt pain before, and it barely fazed him anymore. Living over four decades in a barren post-apocalyptic world hardened even the most optimistic souls. But he didn't relish the situation it created for him and Claire. He'd specifically asked Lainey if he could accompany Claire on the mission so he could protect her. It was a sentimental request, which was quite out of character for him, but he'd become used to that when it came to the violet-haired woman who consumed the majority of his thoughts. He wasn't sure when she'd taken up residence in his brain, but she now lived there constantly, and it was...disconcerting. Yet...*normal* somehow.

On paper, they were opposites in every way. Cyrus, a stoic, practical soldier in his mid-forties who'd done his best to live with honor but had still made drastic mistakes. Claire, the vivacious young woman who was practically a genius and way too optimistic for his cynical demeanor. Their age difference alone was enough for him to keep their relationship platonic. She should be with a younger man—one who still had hopes and dreams, and one who could believe in hers.

But there were other obstacles as well. The trajectory of their lives would always lead down different paths since she was a trained scholar, and he was a fighter to the core of his being. She also wanted a family, and he'd never coveted a partner or children. Although he wasn't averse to having kids, it wasn't something he craved or focused on. Lastly, and perhaps most important, were the mistakes he'd made. Dalton's death still weighed on him when he allowed himself to remember that fateful day. As a soldier, Cyrus had seen his share of death—that was expected. But after he fatally shot the man, he'd questioned the depth of his humanity. After so many years in a barren world, had he lost his ability to weigh the moral consequences of his actions? Claire, on the other hand, was the sweetest, most genuine person he'd ever known, although she did possess a wicked temper. Regardless, they were light-years apart in every aspect of their personalities.

And still, knowing all of that, Cyrus had an irrepressible desire to protect Claire. It rose from an inner calling so intrinsic it was as constant as breathing or blinking. She'd shown him such kindness, teaching him to read and write over the past years at the hub since post-apocalyptic education was nonexistent in their dystopian world. Cyrus had grown up on a compound near what was formerly Scranton, Pennsylvania, and life had been tough. There were a menagerie of settlers there, of all cultures and creeds, and everyone did their part to contribute. Raising livestock, cultivating the crops, sewing clothes—everyone had their job. Education took a back seat to survival, teaching Cyrus skills that would make him an excellent soldier once he left to join the Old Rebellion at seventeen.

Claire had offered to teach him to read and write years ago since she'd been cultivated into a trained scientist by Lewis, the director of the scientific hub, making her one of the few formally educated people on the barren planet. Lewis had recognized her aptitude and exploited it to help his cause, and Cyrus sometimes sensed her resentment at being stuck at the hub. Although educated, Claire had never really made her own choices. For someone as autonomous as Cyrus, it spurred a desire for her to build a life one day over which she could have more control. Perhaps after they prevented the apocalypse, she could find her way to independence.

He'd thought her gesture to teach him kind and immensely enjoyed their sessions. Eventually, he began to crave them as she shared her vibrant, optimistic personality with him. With one smile, she would infuse him with her ever-present energy. They were two people who might have never crossed paths in another life, but in the one they inhabited, her friendship had come to mean so much.

Now that they were stranded in a time that wasn't theirs, it should've been his opportunity to shine; his occasion to assure her that he would ensure her safety at all costs. Unfortunately, his rapidly swelling ankle had other plans.

"Son of a bitch," he muttered, gently pressing the tender flesh with his fingers. "It's almost the size of a grapefruit."

Claire crouched beside him and examined the damage. "Let me see," she murmured, placing her hands on the injury and applying moderate pressure. The sight of her fingers against his deep brown skin stirred longing in his gut, and he clenched his teeth, determined to push it away.

Her touch was so gentle against the pulsing wound, and he emitted a soft hiss, although he couldn't be sure if it was from lust or pain.

"I'm pretty sure all my weight landed on my ankle as it was bent at a ninety-degree angle. Not a great landing."

"You probably have a fracture," she said, eyes narrowed in concentration, "but it's hard to know unless you get an X-ray. Good news? If we made it to 2035, there are X-ray units aplenty."

"Don't you need insurance to see a doctor?" Cyrus asked. "I remember talking to Lewis about how the world worked before the apocalypse. He always was pretty vocal about how the healthcare system in America sucked."

"Yes," she said, sitting on the grass and contemplating. "It would most likely set off red flags if you walked in uninsured to see a doctor. But we do have the fake IDs Zach made. We need to set up our identities in this timeline and establish credit and a paper trail. Once we have that, insurance shouldn't be too much of a hurdle."

"I think we're jumping ahead. We need to find Lainey and Hunter. It's strange they're not here. I hate to send you to the warehouse alone, but I don't know that we have any other choice."

Her lips pursed. "I agree. I have to go check it out and see what the hell happened." She pointed to his smashed ankle. "And you're not going anywhere on this puppy. Let me set up the tent for you and get you situated, and then I'll head to the warehouse."

"I think you should go before the sun gets any lower."

She stood and placed her fists on her hips. "And leave you to set up the tent? When you can't even stand? Um, yeah, not happening. I could be gone for hours, and we need to at least leave you with some shelter, even if it's makeshift."

"I can do it, Claire."

"Please let me help," she said softly.

Nodding, he observed her bend down to pull the tent she'd packed from her bag. The curves of her generous ass strained in her jeans, and Cyrus's fingers dug into the grass. Claire was a curvy woman, and he absolutely adored every single dip and hollow. He found her body extremely sexy and wished like hell he could explore every erogenous zone.

Telling himself to stop staring, he extended his arms. "At least let me put together the frame. I can do that while sitting."

She handed him some of the retractable pieces, and he began to fit them together while she spread out the covering.

Marie and Zach had worked on the tents together. Zach had figured out how to melt down certain rocks to form the plastic-like components that comprised the frame, while Marie had lovingly sewed the canopy from the deer hides Lewis and Cyrus brought back from their hunting excursions over the years. It would provide a place for Cyrus to nurse his wound while Claire went in search of their team.

Once the tent was assembled and Cyrus was situated inside, Claire crouched down to give him a hug. She slipped her arms around his neck, her generous breasts crushing against his chest.

"Be safe, okay? I'm worried since you don't have a gun."

"I'll be fine. I have three knives and years of combat training. Don't worry, Finch." He'd always loved calling her by her last name, the moniker somehow poignant and something shared only between them.

Drawing back, she cupped his cheek. "I'm so sorry you're hurt."

A sharp pang formed in his solar plexus as he noticed the tears glistening in her light green eyes. She was someone who experienced a gamut of emotions on a daily basis and always wore them on her sleeve. For someone as stoic as him, it was perplexing. Cyrus held so much inside and had a reverent respect for her ability to express herself so openly.

"Don't worry about me, Claire," he almost whispered, tucking a strand of hair behind her ear. "I need you to focus on finding the others. I'll be fine."

Nodding, she compressed her lips, looking as if she wanted to say more. After tenderly swiping her thumb across his cheek, she stood and gathered her bag. Giving him one last wave, she exited the tent and zipped it up.

Left alone with his thoughts, Cyrus closed his eyes and railed at the fact she was venturing alone in a world she didn't know. His one mission had been to protect her, and he couldn't even do that. Cursing the unfairness of the situation, he elevated his leg and lay back to count the seconds until her return.

Chapter 3

Twenty-five minutes later, Claire exited the wooded park to the open clearing. She'd kept a steady pace and congratulated herself that she was only slightly out of breath. Was she out of shape? Probably. But she'd always had a healthy appetite and preferred spending time doing other things besides exercise. Crunching numbers with Zach, reading Lainey's mother's old romance novels, and writing poetry while she jammed out to classic rock—those things were *way* more fun than exercise. Acknowledging that life was too short to spend it doing crap you didn't like, Claire forged ahead in search of the warehouse.

Instead, she only saw a large clearing covered with flattened dirt and several yellow bulldozers. Claire had studied the early twenty-first century extensively in anticipation of traveling to 2035 and understood the purpose of the hulking machines. But why were they scattered over what looked to be a newly zoned construction site?

Shrugging her bag from her shoulders, she pulled out the water container and took some hefty swigs as she assessed the expanse. Wiping the wetness from her lips with the back of her arm, she contemplated. Something was off. Where in the hell were Lainey, Hunter, and Luke? How could a massive concrete building not be in the place it was supposed to be?

Struggling to discern the answer, her ears perked as she heard a commotion to her left. Turning, she noticed a pickup truck ambling up the dirt road. When it approached, a man lowered the window, and Claire caught the melody of Eminem's "Lose Yourself" blaring from the speakers before he turned the radio down. Claire absolutely adored music and prided herself on understanding many of the different genres that were popular before the apocalypse. Zach had restored Lainey's mother's old iPod for her, and she'd listened to thousands of songs Mara had downloaded.

"Hi there, ma'am," the man said. "Are you all right? This is an active construction zone, and it's not really safe to be here. I'm the supervisor and was about to head home when I saw you at the top of the hill. Do you need a ride?"

"No, thank you," she said, judging the man safe, although she'd never get into a vehicle with a stranger. "I was hiking in the nearby woods and stumbled upon the site. For some reason, I thought it had been completed."

He shook his head. "No, ma'am, we actually just got our permits about a month ago. We anticipate having the entire industrial park completed by late 2004."

Confusion, sticky and heavy, pervaded Claire's veins. "Wow, uh, that means you'll end up building it pretty quickly, I guess."

"Yeah, two years is pretty fast to build an entire industrial park, but I think we can stay on schedule."

"Right," she said, fingers clenched around her water bottle. "So it's 2002, and you'll build for two years."

The man's eyebrows drew together. "Yep. Since March is nearly over, we'll get some warm weather in April, which will help."

"March 2002," Claire mumbled. "Got it."

"So, um, I need to get home to the wife and kids, ma'am. The sun's going down soon. Are you sure I can't give you a ride?"

"Oh, no, thanks so much," she said, waving him off. "I really appreciate your help. My friends actually set up camp about five-hundred yards into the woods, and they're expecting me. They know I like to venture off and explore. Thanks so much for checking on me. Have a good night!" Claire smiled enthusiastically, hoping to assure him. He gave her a kind smile and a short wave and drove off.

Overcome with realization, Claire dropped to the ground. Running her hand through her hair, she expelled a breath through puffed cheeks. Somehow, she and Cyrus had traveled to late March 2002. It was most likely due to Eli's interference in the bunker and Zach's decision to propel them through the wormhole before the Sphere was seized. Letting the realization sink in, Claire admitted they were royally screwed.

She and Cyrus were stuck over thirty years further in the past than they should be, his ankle was a mess, and they had absolutely no contacts in this timeline. The gravity of their situation threatened to choke her as it sank into every pore and bone in her body.

Steeling herself, Claire pushed to her feet and straightened her spine. Reminding herself that things could be worse, she focused on the positives. She was alive in an era with almost limitless technology, accompanied by a man whom she adored. Claire owed it to both of them to help him heal and figure out a solution to their precarious situation. Drawing on the inner strength she so often doubted but knew existed deep within, Claire slung her bag over her shoulder and began the trek back to Cyrus...and to whatever the future held for them.

* * * *

Cyrus heard rustling outside the tent and knew Claire had returned. She unzipped the fabric and entered, closing it behind her. Darkness was now upon them, and that worried Cyrus. They were stranded in a national park on the outskirts of Washington, D.C., with meager supplies and no connection to the outside world. As his ankle throbbed atop his bag, which he was using to elevate the mangled limb, he glanced at Claire.

Her cheeks were flushed, causing her to look angelic in the flickering light of the candle he'd lit. He'd packed some basic survival items—candles, matches, granola bars—as well as his knives, some clothes, and the fake ID and pre-apocalyptic currency totaling ten thousand dollars Zach had supplied him with. They wouldn't get them far, but they were better than nothing. One lesson he'd learned over the years was that things could always be worse.

Claire appeared nervous as she rubbed her hands over her jean-clad thighs, sitting cross-legged next to him. Concern laced her features as she glanced toward his ankle.

"How's it feeling?"

Cyrus shrugged. "Hurts like a bitch, but nothing I can't handle. Did you find the warehouse? Any sign of Lainey and Hunter?"

"Yeah," she said, biting her lip as she seemed to contemplate her words. "I'm pretty sure we're not going to be meeting up with them."

"Why?"

Peridot-green irises darted between his.

"I found the site where the warehouse should be. A man pulled up in a truck claiming to be the construction manager and proceeded to inform me that it's March of 2002, Cyrus."

Cyrus felt his features draw together. "2002," he muttered.

She nodded. "We traveled back to the wrong time. We're stuck in 2002, and I have absolutely no idea how we're going to navigate that. Lainey and Hunter must've made it to 2035 because they're nowhere to be found, and I'm pretty sure Eli prevented anyone else from coming back. It's just us, Cyrus. We're stranded here."

Cyrus digested the information, comprehending the significance of her words. "We're stuck in 2002."

"Yes," she whispered.

Blowing out a breath, he rubbed his hands over his face. "That's a curveball I didn't see coming."

"I know."

Cyrus noticed her chin quivering ever so slightly. He might not be able to physically help her, but he definitely had the strength to comfort her. Aching to soothe her, he held out his hand.

"Come here, Finch," he said softly. "It's going to be okay."

She grasped on for dear life, letting him draw her to his side and resting her head on his shoulder. Overcome with the smell of her hair and her soft curves pressed against his body, he stroked the silken tresses.

"We're both exhausted and won't be able to do anything if we don't get some rest. Blow out the candle, and let's get some sleep. Everything will look better tomorrow once the sun has risen and we've digested this."

She lifted to douse the candle and then snuggled into his side again. Cyrus closed his eyes, reveling in how perfectly she fit into every crevice of his frame. Placing a soft kiss on her forehead, he caressed her hair.

"I've got you."

"I know," she whispered, sliding her hand over his heart, quietly pounding under his black T-shirt. "If I have to be stuck with anyone, I'm glad it's with you."

Me too...

The words flitted through his brain, poignant and true. Then, giving into exhaustion, he fell asleep with Claire in his arms.

Chapter 4

The next morning, they awoke refreshed and ready to form a plan.

"So I've been thinking," Claire said, returning to the tent after heading outside to relieve herself and brush her teeth. Cyrus had done the same earlier, leaning on Claire for support since he couldn't bear any weight on his ankle. He'd taken shelter behind a tree, wondering how in the hell they were going to get any sort of medical care, especially since his ankle was more swollen than yesterday. "The first thing we need to do is get your ankle set. If it is fractured, we need some sort of cast or molding."

"Lewis said there were emergency rooms in hospitals back in the day where someone could go if they were hurt."

Claire nodded, looking pensive. "I'm worried that will trigger so many disasters we need to avoid. Yes, we have our forged IDs, but we still have no paper trail in this timeline. We could inadvertently spur the staff to call the authorities and get locked up for fraud or all sorts of other things."

"With no one to bail us out," Cyrus said.

"Yeah, I'm not really digging going to jail at the moment."

"I'm open to suggestions. As tough as I am, I do need to address the sprain. The swelling is worrisome."

Her slightly crooked teeth played with her bottom lip as she contemplated. He'd often heard her remark about how she hated her teeth, but they fit together in a jagged puzzle that completed her gorgeous smile. Every time she'd beamed at him over the years, his heart had somehow clicked further into place.

"I'm thinking of some conversations I had with Marie about her mother," she said, eyes narrowed. "She told me her mom was a doctor who treated underserved patients in a financially suppressed section of D.C. I got the impression her mother was kind of a badass, trying to stick it to the man and heal patients the healthcare system wouldn't accept due to lack of insurance or funds."

"That's noble. If it's true, she might be willing to treat me without any documentation."

"Bingo," Claire said, standing. "The question is, how am I going to get you there? There's no way you can put weight on that ankle, and I don't know if you can physically hop all the way to a road where we can find transport to the Brentwood neighborhood. That's where Marie said she grew up."

"If I had crutches, I could hobble along. I hate to send you out there alone again, but it might be best if you try to locate Marie's mom without my dead weight. Maybe she could lend you some crutches so I can make it to a road where we can get a cab."

"It's nice that you want to protect me, but you don't think I'm helpless, do you, chief?"

Cyrus grinned. He'd always liked the nickname used only by Claire, mostly when they shared reading sessions, her instruction always so patient and thorough. "Not at all, Finch. You're tough as nails. I just worry because I care."

Her throat bobbed as she swallowed. "I care about you too, Cyrus. So much." The rasp in her voice shifted something inside his injured body.

"Okay, let's get you to Brentwood then. What was Marie's mom's name?"

"Vivian Elders. I remember because I always thought Vivian was such a pretty name, and Marie took her maiden name back once she divorced her husband."

Cyrus nodded. "Let's pack your bag with essentials and get you on your way. I don't want to push you, but it's better to send you out there while the sun is high. I'll disassemble the tent and pack everything up while you're gone."

"On that ankle?"

He shrugged. "It will give me something to do. It won't be fast or pretty, but I need something to occupy me. Even though it's futile, I'm going to worry every second until you come back, Claire."

"I'll be safe," she said, standing and wiping her hands on her jeans. "It's like a new adventure. How exciting."

Chuckling, he nodded. "Let's get you packed."

Together, they decided on essential supplies, and Claire headed off into a world she didn't know, brave and strong. As Cyrus watched her depart through the open section of the tent, he balanced his fear with the knowledge Claire was resilient enough to accomplish anything she put her mind to.

Chapter 5

It took Claire about two hours to hike out of the park and find a business district. Approaching a row of stores that were situated together, she read the signs. One said "Val's Diner," while another said "Mini Mart" and had a flashing sign that read "Pre-paid Phones for Sale Here."

Her stomach growled, making the decision that she'd need to eat before she did anything. She felt bad leaving Cyrus behind with granola bars while she found a hot meal, but Claire's brain didn't function well when she was hungry. She'd learned this from years of experience and snapping at her beloved team when her belly was empty. Deciding she would eat quickly, she trailed to the diner.

The hostess told her to take any open booth, so she did, opening the menu that looked like a novel. It offered up anything one could imagine: all-day breakfast, meats, cheeses, soups. Claire studied the plastic pages with wide eyes, feeling as if she'd entered utopia. How did people live in a world with unlimited food at their fingertips? Did they even know how fortunate they were? At the hub, they were lucky if Marie baked bread once a week. The chickens that lived out back barely laid any eggs (in Claire's opinion, at least!) and the times when Lewis went fishing in the river and brought home trout were celebrated like national holidays.

"Hi, sweetie," a woman said from above, holding a pen and pad. "What can I get you?"

Claire pointed at the menu. "I can order anything that's listed here?" she asked, almost in disbelief.

"Yep," the waitress said, chomping gum between her teeth. "But don't order the lobster. It's gross. Save that for a fancy place."

"Right." Trailing her finger over the menu, she landed on the French toast special. Marie had made French toast sparingly, as milk and bread took labor to produce, and it had always been Claire's favorite. "I'll take this," she said, mouth watering in anticipation.

Nodding, the server jotted on the pad. "Do you want home fries or French fries and sausage or bacon?"

Bacon? They had so few pigs on the hub, bacon was more valuable than gold in 2075.

"French fries and bacon, please."

"You got it, honey. Coffee?"

"Sure."

Ten minutes later, Claire was embroiled in what was probably the most scrumptious meal of her life. Each bite was savored, eyes closed as she chewed, and when she munched the crispy bacon, she sent a message to the universe, pretty sure she could die without any regrets moving forward. It was that damn good. Darcy, the pretty waitress who'd been serving her, approached with a huge smile on her face.

"Guess it's good?"

"*Ohmygod,*" Claire breathed, shaking her head in wonder. "How do you work here and stay so thin? I'd morph into one of the booths and never leave."

Darcy chuckled and refilled her coffee. "You get tired of it after a while. So are you from here? I haven't seen you before."

Claire shook her head, wiping her fingers on her napkin. "Passing through. I need to buy a pre-paid phone. Is the place next door legit?"

"Yep, it's run by Charlie and his son Hakeem. They're both really nice. Hakeem comes into the diner a lot and always sits in my section. He's a great tipper." Claire noticed the woman's cheeks flush as she grinned.

"Sweet. So you think he'll show me how to use the phone if I buy it? I'm not too savvy on the darn things, actually."

Darcy sighed. "I know. I feel like cell phones are taking over the world. One day, everyone will probably have one. The majority of people I know already do. I still have a beeper and will hold out as long as I can."

Claire mulled her words, realizing this was the point in time where cell phones were just becoming mainstream. "I have a feeling you're right, Darcy. In the not too distant future, those little contraptions are going to run people's lives. They'll end up using them to socialize and date and search the internet. All sorts of things besides just talking on the phone."

Darcy studied her, eyes narrowed. "Well, that seems a bit excessive. How do you date on a phone?"

Claire smiled, remembering everything Lewis and Marie had told her about pre-apocalyptic America. "Honestly, it sounds pretty far-fetched to me too. Forget it. I like a good ol' fashioned person-to-person conversation myself." Reaching into her bag, Claire pulled out some bills. "Can I pay you in cash?"

"Cash is key, sister," Darcy said, pulling out her pad and totaling the bill. "It comes to seven eighty-five. You can pay at the register, but you can leave a tip on the table if you like." She gave Claire a wink. "Nice talking to you. Good luck with the phone."

"Thanks."

Claire left a five-dollar bill on the table, making sure it was one of the older bills printed before 2008 and the introduction of the redesigned five-dollar note. Lewis had proved his genius, making sure to stockpile pre-redesigned notes along with post-redesigned ones in their stash. Although he'd never planned on traveling further back than 2035, the man understood possibilities for making mistakes were endless and postulated there was a small chance the Sphere would malfunction and send them to an incorrect timeline.

"Good lookin' out, Lewis," she mumbled to herself.

As she paid at the register, Darcy yelled an exclamation of thanks to her, waving the bill in the air beside the table. Claire gave her a good-natured salute and headed a few doors down to the mini mart.

Twenty minutes later, after a brief but thorough tutorial from Hakeem, Claire was equipped with a brand new Voicestream pre-paid cell phone. The device was intuitive, and she had a quick mind, so it was actually a breeze to use. Thanking the kind young man, she asked him about Darcy.

"Oh, yeah," he said, smiling sheepishly. "She's so nice. She always takes such good care of us."

"You should ask her out," Claire said. "She seems to really enjoy it when you come into the diner."

Excitement entered his eyes. "Yeah? I thought she had a boyfriend."

"Well, you never know until you ask. I think you should definitely go for it. Thanks for showing me the ropes with the phone!" Breezing out the door into the brisk but fairly warm March day, Claire dialed the number of the cab company Hakeem had given her.

Ten minutes later, a man pulled up in a white checkered taxi, and she was on her way to Brentwood. Since she had no idea where she was going and the taxi driver probably knew the lay of the land, she pressed him for information.

"From what I understand, there's a physician in the Brentwood neighborhood who treats underserved patients. Dr. Vivian Elders. Have you heard of her?"

"Doc Viv?" the man said, smiling in the rearview mirror. "Everybody knows Doc Viv. She helped my Uncle Stuart when he lost his two toes to diabetes and the hospital wouldn't readmit him to fix the infection. Damn moneygrubbing doctors. That's all these hospitals care about nowadays. Except Doc Viv. She'll see you no matter what, money or not. She's a damn angel."

"Sweet. I'd like you to take me to her clinic if possible."

Concern flashed across his features. "Are you hurt, ma'am?"

"No," she said, smiling at his kindness. "But one of my friends is, and I need to consult with her to see if she'll take him on as a patient."

"You'll be in good hands, ma'am," he said, nodding firmly. "Doc Viv ain't never turned down no patient who needs it. Tell her Uncle Stuart's nephew Brandon says hi. She knows me." White teeth flashed as he beamed.

"I sure will, Brandon. Thank you."

A few minutes later, they arrived in front of a dilapidated two-story house. Shingles that had seen better days hung from the roof, and there was a rickety wooden sign that read "Health Clinic." After paying Brandon, Claire tentatively approached, passing an elderly couple slowly exiting the home via the broken and cracked sidewalk. Walking up the front porch stairs, she entered, eyes adjusting to the dim surroundings.

"The sign-in sheet's right here," a girl who appeared to be around nine or ten years old said, sitting behind a counter. Pointing at the clipboard that rested on top, she beckoned to Claire. "Go on and put your name down. It's about a twenty-minute wait right now."

Claire approached the counter, her limbs heavy with recognition as she struggled to breathe. Staring into the girl's hazel eyes, she said, "Marie?"

Marie scowled. "Yeah? Have we met before? I don't remember you."

Flashes of eighty-year-old Marie with her long, white braid and eyes sparkling with mischief flitted through Claire's brain. The woman was a whirlwind on the hub, weathered and gruff from her life experience, but also caring and nurturing. She'd been a guidepost for Claire, calm and steady when emotion clouded her vision.

Feeling her eyes widen, she grabbed the pen and signed her name, her hand shaking at the awesomeness of the moment. Even for an experienced scientist such as Claire, meeting a younger version of another person you knew intimately in a previous timeline was mind-blowing.

"I've walked past the clinic several times and seen you playing in the yard," she said, striving to come up with an explainable scenario. "I've overheard others call your name."

Marie's eyes narrowed, shrewd and contemplative. "Sounds fishy, but we're busy today, so I won't grill you. Have a seat in the waiting room, and Mom will be with you shortly."

"Aren't you supposed to be in school?"

Her tiny shoulders shrugged. "The receptionist is sick, so Mom let me stay home and work the desk today. She pays me seven dollars an hour. I told her it wouldn't be fair if she didn't pay me."

Claire breathed a laugh, realizing Marie possessed a stubborn spirit even as a kid. "Great negotiating."

"Yep," she said, displaying a crooked smile. "Your injury isn't urgent, right? Most people know they have to wait to see Mom."

"I'm actually not the one who's injured. I'm here for a friend. I need to consult with your mom."

"Okay, take a load off. I'll call you when she's ready."

Claire chuckled at her precociousness. "Thanks, Marie."

Lowering to one of the chairs lining the wall of the living room that had been turned into a waiting area, Claire studied the other patients. They were a cross section of every culture and age, with some varying comorbidities she could observe with the naked eye. One older lady had an oxygen tank and a tube attached to her nose. Another man had a cast on his wrist. A younger man had a huge bandage on his forehead, and she guessed he was probably waiting for stitch removal. Eyeing the room, Claire realized she'd stumbled into a microcosm of the culture of the early 2000s. It was really exciting to someone with her voracious mind, and she wanted to learn everything she could about the mysterious new timeframe.

Reaching to her right, she picked up the glossy magazine. The headline read "Bennifer" and there was a picture of a gorgeous brunette and a handsome man with a wide smile. Curious, Claire flipped to the main story. Apparently, Jennifer Lopez and Ben Affleck were huge stars in this timeframe and they'd been given one combined name. Wrinkling her nose, Claire decided that was stupid. Who wanted a mashed-up name? Were people really so lazy that they couldn't say two names? Pondering, she tried it for herself and Cyrus. Clairus. Ew. It sounded ridiculous. She'd keep her own separate name, thank you very much.

After catching up on Bennifer, Britney and Justin, and several other celebrities she'd vaguely heard of, Marie called her name. Claire stood and followed her down a hallway toward the last door. A chestnut-haired doctor sat at a desk scribbling on a chart, and Marie gestured for Claire to sit down in one of the vacant chairs that faced the desk.

"Watch out for this one," Marie said, pointing to Claire with her thumb. "She likes to eavesdrop. Kinda shady, if you ask me." Shrugging, she exited and closed the door.

Dr. Elders smiled at Claire, removing her glasses and rubbing her eyes. Sighing, she chuckled. "My daughter, Marie. She's nine years old going on forty. I can barely keep up with her half the time."

Claire smiled. "She is spirited, for sure. That will come in handy when she becomes an adult and needs to blaze her own path."

"Sure will." Nodding, Dr. Elders relaxed back in her chair. Her eyes narrowed as she studied Claire. "So Marie said you're here to consult with me regarding an acquaintance of yours?"

Claire toyed with her lip, wondering how forthright she should be. "Yes. We're not from here and don't have any insurance. Unfortunately, my friend has hurt his ankle really badly, and I'm afraid it's fractured or broken. I'm hoping you can help him. I would need to borrow some crutches to get him here, Dr. Elders."

"Call me Doc Viv," she said, sitting up in her chair. "I'm happy to help you and..."

"Cyrus," Claire offered.

"Cyrus. Well, yes, I'd be happy to look at his ankle. I have a functioning X-ray machine and can set a cast if needed. Where is he right now?"

"We're camping in Little Falls Stream Valley Park. We don't really have anywhere else to stay."

"Okay, I'll need to help you with that too. No point in healing him if you two have nowhere to stay. Would you be willing to bunk together in a private room? I know someone who might have a vacancy. It's not fancy, but it's clean and functional."

"That would be awesome," Claire said. "We don't really know anyone in Washington D.C."

Doc Viv studied her for a moment. "I think there's more to the story than you're telling me, Claire."

She swallowed thickly. "Honestly, there's a lot more, but it's...complicated."

"Fair enough." Lifting the receiver on her desk, Doc Viv punched some numbers on the keypad. "Paul? Yeah, it's Doc Viv. You still got a vacant room at the house on Cedar Street? How much? Two hundred dollars a month." She arched a brow, and Claire nodded, giving the green light. "Okay. I've got two tenants who'll most likely want to rent it. I'll vouch for them." Holding her hand over the receiver, she whispered, "You have cash, right?"

Claire nodded.

"They'll pay in cash, Paul. Expect them sometime today. I'll give Claire your number. Yep, Claire..."

"Finch."

"Claire Finch," Doc Viv said into the phone. "Thanks. I owe you one."

Hanging up, the doctor gave her a brilliant smile. "Well, Claire Finch, I think we're on our way. Let's find you some crutches."

Chapter 6

Claire took a cab back to the park and trailed through the woods, crutches in hand. She found Cyrus sitting by the packed-up tent, a smile curving his lips. After helping him to his feet, they slung their packs across their shoulders, Cyrus hoisted the crutches under his arms, and they headed toward civilization. Once they were at the clearing where the forest met the road, Claire called a cab.

When they reached Doc Viv's office, Marie stared up at them from behind the desk. "Have I met you before too?" she asked, eyes narrowed as she gazed at Cyrus.

"I don't think so," he said, feigning contemplation. "If we had, I would've remembered." Glancing at Claire, he muttered, "Feisty as hell even at this age."

Claire nodded and gave him a knowing smile.

"What was that?" Marie asked.

"Nothing," Claire said, waving a hand. "Can your mom take a look at his ankle now?"

Marie peered over the counter and gave a low whistle. "Looks really bad, man. Let's get you into X-ray stat." Standing, she walked around the desk and led the way to the X-ray room.

Ten minutes and three X-rays later, Claire and Cyrus sat in front of Doc Viv as she finished up a phone call. "Listen, Alex," she said, frustration lining her features, "you're going to operate on my patient, or I'm going to tell Frannie about the medical sales rep who brings you private lunches every Friday. I think we both know what type of business is being conducted in those meetings." Holding her hand over the receiver, she shot Claire and Cyrus a droll glare. "He's an ass," she said, shaking her head. "Give me a minute."

Nodding, they let the man on the phone finish his tirade.

Doc Viv nodded into the phone. "Yes, Alex, I'll take responsibility for Mr. Chambers' post-surgery care. Thank you. You're a saint. Call me afterward."

Hanging up the phone, she sighed, resting her forearms on the desk. "Sorry. Alex is a surgeon who has a nasty habit of only operating on people with stellar insurance. Unfortunately, my patient needs an emergency procedure, so I had to get a bit randy. Honestly, that was pretty fun." Wrinkling her nose, she winked. "Okay," she said, picking up the X-rays and walking toward the viewing light. Sticking the film in, she illuminated the image. "See here?" she asked, pointing at the picture of Cyrus's ankle. "You've got hairline fracture, Mr. Montgomery. It was probably already compromised when you fell on it. That dislocated the ankle, causing the entire area to swell."

"Call me Cyrus, please," he said, eyes narrowing as he stared at the picture. "What's the prognosis?"

"I'll wrap it for you and put an air cast on it. You'll need to elevate it and use crutches for several weeks. I'm also going to prescribe you Percocet to alleviate the swelling and discomfort. I can't believe you're not more affected by the pain, honestly. It's got to be severe."

Cyrus exhaled. "It's not a bed of roses, Doc, but I've lived through worse."

Her eyebrow arched. "Tough cookie. I like it. Paul has secured a room on Cedar Street for you. The painkiller will make you loopy and drowsy, so it would be best if Claire can take care of you for a while until you stop taking it."

"I'll be right by his side," Claire said, slipping her hand into Cyrus's and giving a squeeze.

He grinned and squeezed back, causing Claire's heart to constrict.

Doc Viv's irises traveled between them as her expression softened. "You two have a bond. It's nice to see. I think Claire will be an excellent nurse. Let's get this party started. Cyrus, hop on the exam table."

Once his ankle was set and secured in an air cast and they were armed with a prescription, they headed to the pharmacy Doc Viv had recommended. It was run by a nice man named Joseph who filled the prescription and let them pay in cash. Prepared with everything they needed, Claire and Cyrus headed to their new temporary home.

Paul's rental home was comprised of three stories, four rooms on each floor. As they ambled into their second-floor room, Claire noted the functionality. There was a kitchenette in the corner with a mini-fridge, a hot plate, and a microwave. The small living room led to a bedroom with a queen bed with freshly washed sheets.

"There are coin laundry machines in the basement," Paul said, handing Claire two keys. She gave him two hundred dollars, and he smiled. "This will cover you for a month. Towels and other necessities are in the closet. If you need anything else, just page me."

"Will do," Claire said. "Thanks, Paul."

He nodded and closed the door as he departed.

"Well," Claire said, rubbing her palms on her thighs. "Let's get you comfortable and get that ankle elevated. Once you're set, I'll head to the store and get us some food."

She gave Cyrus privacy so he could use the bathroom and change. Knocking softly on the bedroom door, she waited for his muffled, "Come in."

He was lying on the bed, grunting as he shifted two pillows under his ankle.

"Here," she said, rushing to his side. Urging him to lie back, she fluffed the pillows and positioned his leg. "That should be better." Her eyes roved over his firm body, clad in a T-shirt and boxers, and her palm prickled from the coarse hairs she touched as she maneuvered his ankle. Sitting on the bed, she cupped his cheek.

"Do you need anything?"

He shook his head, and Claire noticed his glassy eyes. "I feel weird," he said.

She breathed a laugh. "Doc Viv said the painkiller would make you feel loopy. It's okay, Cyrus. You need to rest. That's the best thing you can do right now."

Lifting his hand, he covered hers as it cupped his cheek. His hand dwarfed hers, his russet skin a striking contrast. Longing curled in her gut, and she felt a contraction at her core; a deep yearning she only felt with Cyrus.

"I'm sorry you have to take care of me," he said, a stark genuineness in his coffee-colored irises. "I'm supposed to take care of you."

"We're a team," she almost whispered. "We take care of each other."

His eyes darted between hers. "Claire," he breathed.

"Yes?" she said, running her thumb over his cheek.

Slow, measured breaths exited his lungs. "I'm so tired," he finally said, eyelids drooping.

"I know. Go to sleep. I'll be here when you wake up."

He mumbled something unintelligible, and she grinned, realizing she might get a window into the serious soldier's soul now that he was taking medicine that lowered his ability to inhibit his thoughts. Would she finally discern what he was truly thinking when he studied her with his silent gaze? How interesting. Biting her lip, she pondered as he fell asleep. Was it possible he felt even once ounce of the crippling desire she felt for him? God, but that would be amazing.

Shaking her head, Claire silently told herself to exit la-la land. She and Cyrus were stranded in a strange timeline with nearly insurmountable obstacles ahead of them. Desire, existent or not, was very low on the priority list.

Noting the cadence of Cyrus's breathing, she leaned down and gently kissed his forehead. After securing their place and loading her bag, she locked the door behind her and headed into the world to buy some food.

<h1 style="text-align:center">Chapter 7</h1>

The next morning, Claire's body was sore from sleeping on the lumpy living room couch. In the small kitchen, she unwrapped the sausage biscuits she'd ordered from the McDonald's a block away. Setting them on the plates she found in the cabinet above the hot plate, she strode into the bedroom.

"Rise and shine, chief," she said, smiling as she sat on the bed. "One for you, and one for me."

"Thanks," Cyrus huffed as he positioned the pillows against the headboard and settled in. Taking the plate, he consumed a bite and closed his eyes, chewing in ecstasy. "Man, this is so good."

"It's heaven," Claire said, the words jumbled from the food in her mouth. It was probably rude to talk with food in her mouth, but she'd eaten in front of Cyrus so many times. If he wasn't used to her habits by now, he never would be.

"What?" she asked, swallowing as he smiled at her.

"You've got a..." He motioned toward his own bottom lip.

"Damn it," she said, laughing and running her hand over her lip until she found the wayward speck of food. "You always catch me with food all over my mouth. So gross. Sorry."

"It's funny, Finch," he said, taking another bite as he scrutinized her.

"You know," she said when the silence grew heavy, "you look at me weird like that sometimes, and I have no idea what you're thinking."

His features fell, becoming slightly more serious, and she felt her eyebrows draw together. "Yeah, that's it," she said, circling her palm over her face. "You're doing it now. What the hell are you thinking?"

He chewed methodically, causing Claire to postulate he was drawing out the task to form his answer. After a few moments, he said, "I just think you're cute, Claire. That's all."

"Yeah?" she asked, attempting to stay calm like a normal person who'd been given a compliment by the man they'd had a million lust-filled dreams about. "I figured you leaned more toward sex goddesses like Alora."

A laugh escaped his throat as he ingested the last bit of the sandwich. Swallowing it, he licked his lips, the image of his wet tongue causing a gush of moisture to rush between her jean-clad thighs.

"Alora is an amazing woman and very beautiful. But so are you. Women are all so beautiful in their own unique ways. Us men are very lucky."

She took his empty plate, stacking it upon hers on the bedside table. "That's a nice thing to say. I wish I was beautiful."

"Hey," he said, his fingers encircling her forearm and drawing her to sit beside him on the bed again. "You're gorgeous, Claire. I mean it." He squeezed her arm.

"Thank you," she whispered, unable to say more because her heart now resided in her throat, furiously pumping blood through her shaking frame.

His lips formed a smile as he nodded. When he released her arm, the cool rush of air slapped against her skin, and she longed to feel his warmth again. "So," he said, straightening against the pillows. "Now that I'm on the mend, we've got to figure out what the hell to do."

Claire glanced down at his ankle propped high on a pillow. It was still swollen but did look a bit better.

"I'm open to ideas. I found Doc Viv, so now it's your turn to come up with a plan. This ol' noggin is tired." She gently tapped her knuckles against her forehead.

Chuckling, his features drew together. "I've been thinking. There are a few things we need to figure out. Most importantly, is Lainey going to come for us? That would mean she somehow builds a Sphere in 2035 and travels back here to get us. What do you think?"

Claire pursed her lips and squinted at the ceiling. "I don't know. Eli raided the bunker during our transport, so the logical conclusion would be that the others are still in 2075. If that's the case, Lainey will stop at nothing to rescue them. I'd bet anything she's in 2035 furiously searching for a way to recreate the Sphere so she can find all of us at our various points in space-time."

"I agree. Would she track down Lewis to have him help her?"

Claire chewed her bottom lip, contemplating. "No," she said, features drawn together in speculation. "She'd most likely track down Nelson. Lainey is very respectful of space-time continuum paradoxes, and she probably wouldn't want to come into contact with Lewis unless absolutely necessary."

"But she plans to come into contact with her grandfather."

"Yes, but she never met President Randolph and has no affinity toward him. Lewis is the person she loved above all others. Making contact with someone you were so emotionally tied to in a different timeline can have devastating consequences."

"Okay, let me think," Cyrus said, rubbing his chin with his fingers. A slight stubble had started to grow, black with patches of white, and Claire thought it extremely sexy. What would it feel like to have that stubble scrape the curve of her breast as he sucked her nipple between his lips?

"Claire?" he said, waving his hand.

"Sorry, missed what you said." *Because I was imagining sexy times with you on top of this hard-as-hell mattress.* Who gave a damn when his body could cushion the stiffness of the mattress beneath her?

"Okay, I have no idea what planet you've traveled to, but I need you with me, Claire," his deep baritone intoned.

Shaking her head, she rid it of the madness. "Sorry. Momentary space-out. I'm here."

"Would you be able to recreate the Sphere? You worked on it for years."

"I don't think so," Claire said, shoulders lifting in a resigned shrug. "I'm a pretty good physicist but not nearly as competent as Lainey. I'm really great with math and equations, but she understands the nuances of time travel theories better than anyone. Plus I'd need access to nuclear power and a whole host of other equipment."

Cyrus nodded as he pondered.

"But," she said, holding up a finger, "we do have the luxury of knowing the future. It's possible Lainey will come back for us, but in the meantime, why don't we try to do some good while we're stuck here?"

"I'm listening."

"I mean," she said, leaning back and resting her palm on the bed, "our entire goal has been to prevent the New Establishment from destroying the world. We don't want to do anything drastic like kill President Randolph. First, because we'd be murderers, but second, we need ensure Lainey is able to confront him in 2035. Drastic changes in this decade could have severe consequences for her mission in the future."

Cyrus's expression grew morose, and she slid her hand over his wrist.

"Hey, you okay?"

"Yeah, just got lost for a sec," he said, staring at her hand as it covered his skin.

Claire understood he was recalling Dalton's death and the guilt he still carried from it. Cyrus had been tasked with transporting the traitor to Solera, and halfway through the journey, Dalton had stolen the knife from his belt. A scuffle had commenced, and Cyrus had fired a fatal bullet into the man's heart.

Claire sat still, wishing she knew how to comfort him. Cyrus was quite impassive at times and rarely spoke about his last fateful encounter with Dalton. When he did, the regret was evident.

"You know can always talk to me, Cyrus."

"Thanks." The emotion all but disappeared as he seemed to effectively push it away. "Let's move on. It's pointless to discuss things we can't change. So we're both on board with not murdering any of the younger versions of the early New Establishment leaders in this timeline."

"On board for not murdering!" she teased, holding up a finger. "Phase One complete." His lips formed a grin, and her muscles released some of their tension. "Seriously, though, although we don't want to harm them, we could do some reconnaissance. President Randolph was sixty-two when he detonated the nukes in 2035. That would make him almost thirty years old in 2002. We could track him down and figure out what makes him tick. If we can discover some weaknesses, that could be valuable information if Lainey does come for us. We could use it to possibly manipulate his actions in 2035."

"I like it," Cyrus said, eyes narrowed as an eyebrow arched. "Pretty clever. Learning your opponents' weaknesses is key to taking them down."

"And it will be fun! We'll be like old-timey detectives in those movies Mara used to show me on her old flash drives. We need a name! Montgomery and Finch, P.I.'s for Hire. But we could use the actual Pi symbol in the name, like this." Reaching over, she grabbed the pad and pen on the bedside table and scrawled, showing him her masterpiece: **Montgomery and Finch, π's for Hire.**

He gave her a droll look, and she snickered.

"What? You already know I'm a science dork. It's so cute!"

"I'll leave the name up to you, but reconnaissance I can do. Let's figure out this bastard's playbook and use it to help Lainey."

Claire bit her lip, a question filtering through her mind. "What if she doesn't come back for us?"

Cyrus blinked slow and steady as he considered. "Let's give her some time. We'll focus on gathering intel while we wait. After a few weeks, if she doesn't show, we'll need to reassess."

"We might be stuck here."

"We might," he said, tilting his head. "If that's the case, I'll make sure to set you up for a full life, Claire. One in which you can thrive and have everything you've ever wanted."

I just want you. The sentiment roared through her brain, true on every level. "And how do you know what I want?" she teased.

"I've heard you tell Lainey about your desire to settle down and have a family one day. I'll help you establish a life in which you can get started on that path."

Her eyes darted between his. "Don't you want a family? People who love you, and who you can lean on when things are tough?"

"No," he said, gaze lowering. "I've always done fine on my own. I don't really think about those things."

She was silent for a moment. "I thought everyone at least contemplated those things every once in a while."

"Protecting everyone at the hub was always my first priority," he said, his gaze reclaiming hers. "That consumed most of my thoughts. But I can see why you aspire to have a family. You're young and have so much life ahead of you."

"All right, old man," she said, rolling her eyes. "You're forty-three, not ninety, and that means, logically speaking, you have over half your life left. Let's not get all gloom and doom, okay?"

Chuckling, he nodded. "Okay. Before we do anything, I'm going to have to let my ankle heal. I think a few more days will do it, and then I can at least amble around on crutches."

"Agreed." Standing, she gathered the plates and smiled down at him. "Ready for another pain pill?"

He grimaced. "Those things make me loopy as hell. I can handle the pain."

"Okay, tough guy. We'll see as the day goes on. In the meantime, I'm going to go explore a bit. I need to find a laptop and figure out how to use it. Internet in this time was mostly dial-up, so I think I can buy a modem and use it through the phone line. We'll need to hook up phone service. There's a lot I can do while you heal."

"I can help. I'm obviously not great at computer stuff, but I can do other tasks. I can read through any documents you find about President Randolph."

"That would be awesome," she said, excited their lessons had paid off. "Let me get crackin' and I'll check on you before I leave. If you need a pain pill, let me know. I mean it."

"Yes, ma'am," he said with a salute.

Giving him a wink, she headed to the kitchen to wash the dishes and begin her first day as senior partner of **Montgomery and Finch, π's for Hire.**

Chapter 8

By the time the sun set low on the horizon, Claire had completed a plethora of tasks. She'd gone to a Radio Shack and purchased a modem and laptop, feeling confident in how to use them after a brief tutorial from the salesman. While Cyrus rested in the bedroom, she called the local phone company and set up an account in her name. It would help establish a paper trail and create a credit history if she ended up needing one down the road. Once the modem was set up, she connected the ethernet cable to the laptop and got to work.

Edward James Randolph was a local Washington D.C. council member from Ward 2, one of the most affluent wards in the district. He lived in Georgetown with his wife and two-year-old son Lewis. There were many news articles about his rise to prominence as a local politician due to his positions on entitlement programs and the recently passed Patriot Act. Councilman Randolph had strong views, which had ensured an overwhelming victory in the last election. He had done several interviews in which he spoke about his belief that an overarching government, headed by men who ran things with a systematic and orderly approach, was best for the people. Those who didn't agree didn't deserve to live under the government that offered them protection and peace.

There were several councilmembers who opposed him, and from the articles she read, it seemed the council meetings were sometimes heated. Was this the beginning of the New Establishment, all these decades removed from 2035? Had these tiny seeds gestated and grown into beliefs that eventually caused the apocalypse?

Exhaling a heavy breath, Claire let the information wash over her. Wanting to share it with Cyrus, she set the laptop aside and knocked softly on the barely cracked door.

"Cyrus?"

He grunted in response, and she trailed into the room, sensing immediately that something was wrong. His skin was slick with sweat under his T-shirt and boxer shorts, and his breathing was slightly labored.

Rushing to his side, she sat on the bed and placed her hand on his wet forehead.

"You're burning up," she said, concern flooding her veins. "Why didn't you call for me?"

"Didn't want to bug you. I thought I could sleep it off."

Frustrated, her features constricted. "You need to communicate with me, Cyrus. I can't do this without you."

"Sorry, Finch," he muttered, the remorse in his eyes softening her. "I hate that I'm not the one taking care of you. This fucking sucks."

She smiled even though her heart was pounding with worry and ran her thumb over his cheek. "That it does. Let me call Doc Viv. I'll be right back."

Grabbing her cell from the table beside the couch, she called the number the kind doctor had given her.

"Hello?"

"Hi, Doc Viv. It's Claire Finch. I'm so sorry to bother you."

"No worries, Claire. How's Cyrus doing?"

"Not good, unfortunately. He has a fever and is sweating profusely."

"Hmm..." The woman seemed to contemplate. "His body's been through a lot. It could be a cold or it could be an infection. Do me a favor, go look at his ankle. Are there any open wounds or sores?"

Claire trailed into the room, silently asking permission to touch Cyrus's ankle. When he nodded, she rotated it atop the pillow.

"Nothing that I can see, Doc."

"Good. I'm still worried there might be some sort of infection. I'm going to call in an antibiotic prescription to the pharmacy. He'll need to take it for ten days. How's he doing on the Percocet?"

"He hates the side effects. Says it makes him feel super woozy."

"Well, that's too bad. I want him to take one a day for at least three days. Lessening the pain is going to help him sleep better, and sleep will help him heal. Taking Percocet concomitantly with antibiotics has been shown to increase the side effects, so he's probably going to feel more disconnected and unsteady. Let him know it will pass once he stops taking the pain pill. After three days, he can go off it, but Mr. Tough Guy needs a break from the discomfort. Tell him Doc Viv is putting her foot down."

Claire chuckled. "Will do."

"Keep me posted. The prescription should be ready in an hour."

"Thank you, Doc. We're so appreciative of everything."

"No prob at all. Take care." The phone clicked, and Claire headed back to sit beside Cyrus.

"Well, chief, you're getting antibiotics, and Doc Viv says you have to take the pain pill for three days minimum."

His jaw clenched. "I hate the way it makes me feel."

"I know, but she's the expert, and I need you well. I'll take care of you. Promise. You trust me, don't you?"

Wary eyes darted between hers. "Yes."

Smiling, she nodded. "A week from now, this will all be over. In the meantime, I can take care of you and tell you what I dug up on President Randolph."

He nodded, exhaustion lining his features, and Claire's heart squeezed in her chest. She would never forgive herself if his health worsened. Resolved to help him heal, she urged him to take a Percocet, thrilled when he reluctantly agreed, and then headed to the pharmacy to grab the antibiotics.

* * * *

Cyrus concentrated on the awful sounds permeating his wearied brain. Claire sat above him, singing what sounded like one of Mara's old classic rock songs she'd stored on the iPod Zach had refurbished. He couldn't tell since Claire was a terrible singer, but he appreciated the effort she put into nursing him.

Gazing at her through slitted lids, he struggled to breathe as she loomed over him. Not from pain—that would never compromise his breathing, for Cyrus had felt much pain in his life. The struggle was borne from her beauty; the essence of everything that was Claire.

Her violet hair hung loose, brushing the top of her arm, as she gently blotted his clammy forehead. Her features were laced with concern as the nostrils of her button nose slightly flared. Clear eyes glimmered with fear...and determination...and...*love*. How had he not seen it before? Cyrus considered himself an observant man. He'd seen flashes of longing in Claire's expression and always deemed them evidence of a harmless crush, but there was no mistaking the tender strokes of her hand upon his brow.

The woman he'd fallen for due to her generous heart and accepting spirit loved him back, although it would be selfish to accept it. Claire was still so young and had been sheltered from many of the harsh realities of their dystopian world. Cyrus felt she should be with someone who could spout science to her as they worked together to better the planet. Cyrus preferred protection and military strategy to science—another glaring difference between them.

And yet, even as he acknowledged how dissimilar they were, he wanted her. He craved her silken skin and generous curves wrapped around every inch of his body. Visions of her flooded his brain: Claire limp with arousal, mouth open in a silent scream, as he kissed every dimple and hollow.

Those guileless eyes locked with his, and her lips curved as she ran the cloth down his face to caress his cheek. Overwhelmed with the need to touch her, his eyes fell to her breasts. The twin globes called to him from the V of her T-shirt, the creamy skin beckoning for his fingers...his lips...his tongue...

Lifting his arm, he placed the tips of his fingers ever so gently against the curve of her breast. She gasped, body frozen, as her eyes grew wide. The pulse at her neck fluttered, and Cyrus would've chuckled at her shocked expression if his throat wasn't closed from desire.

Gently, he traced a pattern over the smooth skin. Her breathing hitched, and the mounds trembled under his touch as they expanded and contracted to the rhythm of her breaths. Slowly, his index finger circled, showing her his intent to repeat the action around her nipple. Green irises searched his, questioning but clear. Emboldened by the arousal in the wide orbs, he slowly slid his fingers under her shirt and bra, cupping her breast. Yearning to see the trembling globe, he pushed the clothing aside, baring her to his heated gaze.

The pink bud of her nipple was ruddy and tight, causing Cyrus to grow rock hard in his boxer briefs. Even through his opioid-induced haze, he felt such aching desire for her. Jaw clenched as his cock strained against his abdomen, he ran his thumb over the tight little bud.

"Cyrus." The high-pitched plea was laced with yearning. Although she was so young and vibrant—an eternal optimist to his stoic pragmatism— he reveled in the fact she wanted him despite their differences and rather large age gap.

Bringing his thumb and forefinger to surround her nipple, he squeezed, testing to see her response. Her mouth fell open, wet lips allowing an arousal-laden breath to exit as she closed her eyes. Holding tight, he twisted the nub, wondering if she would like the thrill of the slightly painful twinge. Cyrus enjoyed exhibiting a certain amount of dominance during sex, and he understood pleasure and pain in the right combination could be magnificent. Would Claire appreciate the same things? Or would it be one more reason a romantic relationship between them would never work?

When she opened her eyes, Cyrus almost groaned at the blazing lust that simmered in the glassy depths. Setting the damp cloth on the bedside table, she glided over his body, anchoring a hand on each side of his shoulders. Gaze locked with his, she lowered her breast to his mouth.

Cyrus's lips searched for her like a beacon in the coldest, darkest night. The little minx trailed the tight bud over his suddenly parched lips, circling, the ruddy texture of her nipple heaven against his sensitive skin. Unable to take the torture, he extended his tongue, licking the tip before he sucked her into his mouth.

"*Oh, god,*" she breathed, eyes closing in pleasure before opening to lock with his. She moaned his name as he milked her nipple, tugging and releasing while creating suction with his tongue against the quivering underside. Her frame trembled above him, the tips of her fragrant hair gently brushing his face. Curious to see her reaction, he lightly clamped his teeth around the nub, pulling it from her body. A flush crossed her skin, turning it a sultry shade of red, and his cock twitched. Would her deepest place flush with arousal too as he ran his tongue over every wet inch? Betting it would, he struggled to retain control. If he wasn't careful, he would end up dragging her to the mattress, opening those thick, sexy thighs, and burying himself in her sweet warmth.

Unable to deny himself, he tugged her shirt down, baring her other breast, and kissed a trail toward it. Groaning, he took her nipple into his mouth, overcome with the smell and taste of her. He'd had many dreams about tasting Claire, and this moment surpassed them all. She mewled, hands clenching his bald head where tiny hairs had started to sprout, and shuddered above him. Understanding he was playing with fire, Cyrus allowed himself one more pull of the delectable tight bud before pulling her close and burying his face between her breasts.

She stilled, panting above him, as he inhaled her honeyed scent. Nuzzling into the crevice of her ample bosom, he let the joy wash over him. He never would've touched her if his defenses weren't down due to the side effects of the pain medicine, but now that he had, he might as well enjoy it before he pushed her away.

They had no future. Cyrus understood this to the depths of his bones. The greatest gift he could give her, if Lainey truly wasn't able to come back and save them, was the ability to go forth in this timeline and find happiness. She would thrive in a university setting, surrounded by others who shared her brilliant mind, and settled with a younger man who shared her dreams of family and children. Already mourning the loss, he gently pushed her away.

"Cyrus?" she called, and his heart twitched at the disappointment in her voice.

"I'm sorry," he rasped, reaching to tug her bra and shirt over her gorgeous breasts. His hands felt clumsy, and his eyelids felt like they had weights attached to them. Giving into the drowsiness, he nuzzled his nose in the valley of the luscious globes.

She shifted atop him, maneuvering to her side while his face was still buried in her fragrant skin. *You have to let her go...* The words trailed through his drug-induced brain, but he was unable to heed them. Soft fingers soothed the smooth skin of his head.

"Shh," she soothed, stroking him as he drifted through the wondrous experience of being in her loving embrace.

Darkness finally overtook him, and he relaxed into the abyss, realizing a true moment of peace for the first time in so very long.

Chapter 9

Claire hummed as she scrambled the eggs in the pan atop the hot plate. Smiling, she immersed herself in the images from the previous evening. Cyrus pulling her close...kissing her breasts...holding her so tight she couldn't tell where his body ended and hers began. Sighing, she bit her lip, unable to control her grin as she recalled the experience. It had been one of the most intimate moments of her life, shared with Cyrus, whom she adored.

Claire had only had one sexual partner in her three decades on the planet. She'd met Nathan when she was seventeen and accompanying Lewis on an excursion to visit some distant cousins at Terrum. At nineteen, Nathan had seemed so worldly to her. His father had passed years before, and he took care of his mother and younger sister on their farm at the outskirts of the compound. She would sneak over from Lewis's cousins' home, situated next door, and listen to the handsome young man tell stories from all the soldiers who'd passed through. The tales were so exciting to Claire, who'd lived at the hub for years and found it quite boring.

One night, Nathan had kissed her as her heart thrummed in her chest. Curious and filled with teenage lust, she'd let him push her to lie atop the soft straw in the barn that housed the horses. There, on a warm summer night, she'd lost her virginity. It had been sweet and clumsy, and Claire often wondered if she'd ever have the opportunity to make love to someone again. The hub hadn't afforded her many willing suitors, and eventually, she'd become so enamored with Cyrus she doubted she would ever want anyone but him. Frustrating, since he was the hottest man on the planet, and she'd convinced herself he'd never desire someone like her—basic and moderately attractive at best.

But last night, everything had changed. For the first time, Claire had seen the aching arousal she felt for Cyrus reflected in his gorgeous eyes. They'd shone so brightly, and he'd sent more sparks of desire through her body with his lips upon her breast than she'd felt during her entire awkward experience with Nathan. If he could set her body on fire with a few swipes of his tongue across her nipple, imagine what he could do if he kissed her most intimate place...or made love to her as she stared into his deep brown irises...

Shaking her head, Claire dispersed salt and pepper onto the eggs she'd scooped onto the plates. Reminding herself Cyrus had been in a drug-induced stupor, she told herself not to get too excited. What if he didn't even remember what happened between them? Good lord, she'd probably die. Yep, just dig herself a hole, crawl in, and never come out.

Grabbing two forks from the drawer, her lips curled as she recalled holding him against her quivering body. He'd fallen asleep in her arms as she'd softly stroked his head, his warm breath skating across the sweat-covered hollow between her breasts. God, she wanted so badly to fall asleep with him like that every night for the rest of her life. Preferably, when he was sober enough to choose to sleep with her.

A loud clank sounded from the bedroom, and her head snapped. Rushing to the room, she found the bed empty and approached the open adjoining bathroom door. Cyrus was standing on his good leg, leaning over the green bathtub as he adjusted the faucet controls.

"Why are you out of bed?" she asked, alarmed.

"No more," he said, his frustration emanating through the small bathroom. "No more pain pills, and no more lying around. I feel better today and refuse to live as an invalid. I'm taking a bath, and I'm going to help you surveil Randolph."

"Okay," she said, taking a hesitant step toward him and placing her palm across his forehead. "You don't feel feverish anymore. That's a good sign."

He nodded, his face an impassive mask. Removing her hand, her teeth toyed with her bottom lip as she struggled to discern whether he remembered their sexy shenanigans the previous evening.

"I'm sorry," he said, closing his eyes as he shook his head. "It's fuzzy, but I remember touching you and...kissing you last night... I...well, I'm sorry." Opening his eyes, they locked onto her. "I hope we're still okay."

"Of course, we're okay," she said, her heart slightly breaking at the regret simmering in his gaze.

"I'll make sure that doesn't happen again. We need to stay focused on the task at hand. My one goal is to keep you safe until Lainey comes for us.

And if she doesn't, I'll set you up for a life where you can thrive. Nothing is more important to me."

"I thrive when I'm with you, Cyrus," she rasped, on the verge of tears.

His expression was devoid of any emotion, causing her to want to melt into the floor. "Let me take a bath, and we'll focus on the mission. That's where I want to place my energy right now."

She nodded, backing toward the door so she could escape before the tears fell. "I made eggs. They're on the counter. I'm going to head outside and get some fresh air."

A flash of remorse skirted across his face before it disappeared. "Okay."

Swallowing the lump that now sat firmly in her throat, she strode out into the early spring day. Finding a soft patch of grass outside the house, she sat beside the withered tree struggling to balance her frayed emotions.

* * * *

Cyrus sat in the lukewarm water, cursing himself a thousand different ways. He'd awoken to the knowledge he'd lost control with Claire the previous night. Scowling, he washed his body, wishing he could wash away the scorching memories. They burned his brain along with the sentiment he'd seen in her stunning eyes. Sighing, he scraped the cloth over his body.

His ankle was now the size of a large apple. Better, but not ideal. Still, he'd realized when he woke up in a pool of sweat from his breaking fever that he was done with the Percocet. Doctor's orders or not, there was no way in hell he'd allow that loss of control again. Claire had purchased some ibuprofen at the store, and the label said it reduced swelling, so he'd take that and suck up the pain. He was a damn soldier after all and had dealt with much worse over his long career.

Popping the plug from the drain, the water drained as he struggled to stand. Reaching for the towel, he dried himself off as he rested all his weight on his good leg. After several minutes of careful maneuvering, he used the crutches to amble back to the bed and dress. Feeling refreshed, he hobbled to the window, observing Claire.

Purple hair flitted in the wind as she sat so very still by a tree beside the house. He'd hurt her this morning, the knowledge threatening to shatter the heart he kept so carefully guarded. But it had been necessary—something his practical mind understood. It was better to shatter her illusions about him now rather than let her long for something that could never be. Lifting his hand, he gently rested the pads of his fingers against the glass.

"I'm sorry," he whispered, yearning to comfort her.

Closing his eyes, he allowed himself one more moment with the memory. Her luscious nipple pressed against his tongue as she breathed his name, drawing him in. Straightening, he lifted his lids, shoulders set. *Enough.* Time was precious, especially in their situation, and he wouldn't spend it on pointless musings. Burying the images deep within, he committed to locking them away.

In the meantime, he could spend every ounce of his energy helping her dig up dirt on Randolph. Smiling, he remembered how adorable she'd looked when she postulated the name of their new P.I. firm. She'd seemed excited to embark on the mission, and he longed to see that sparkle in her eyes again.

Placing the crutches under his arms, he ambled outside to begin the task of surveilling Edward Randolph with the woman whose happiness he was determined to ensure.

Chapter 10

Claire hugged her knees as the early spring breeze blew a strand of hair between her lips. Swiping it away, she took some deep breaths, reigning in her emotions. A bug crawled on the tree beside her, scampering around, perhaps searching for food, and her lips twitched. The little critter reminded her a bit of herself at the hub, which she was surprised to realize she didn't miss at all.

Of course, she was truly thankful Lewis had taken her in after her parents died when she was a teenager. Their dystopian world was dangerous, and she'd been safe at the hub, luckier than most. But she'd often flitted around at the compound struggling to find her place, much like the tiny creature scampering over the bark.

Lewis had recognized her incredible aptitude when she was still a child. She was a distant cousin of his and Lainey's, and Lewis visited them often. Claire sometimes wondered if he took more of an interest in her because of her intelligence. He spent hours during each visit instructing her on math, geometry, calculus, and physics, and his amber eyes would sparkle each time she successfully solved an equation. As an awkward child who didn't possess a ton of confidence, she'd basked in his praise. They only grew closer once she moved into the hub.

But Lewis pushed her, sometimes to the point where she resented him when he told her they didn't have time to go fishing because they needed to crunch numbers, or when he scolded her for wanting to write poetry in her journal instead of using the time more wisely to learn the computer programs Zach had developed. Zach's voracious desire to learn everything and help the cause had always been so much greater than hers. Her dear friend had somehow sensed that and would tease her, making the menial tasks fun. Smiling, Claire realized how much she missed him. How much she missed everyone at the hub. But she didn't miss the hub itself, and she sure as hell didn't mourn not having to dedicate every waking second to saving the world.

Guilt consumed her knowing Lainey and the others were out there, possibly fighting for their lives. But the sentiment was there, buried deep in her heart, and true on every level. If she could create a life for herself in which she never heard the words "Sphere" or "time travel" again, she certainly wouldn't mind.

She'd evolved into a background character there; someone who had no control over her own life, although she was content. Food and friendship were supplied as long as she contributed. That had been enough for so long, but what if she could create something more? As her fingers fidgeted in her lap, Claire envisioned rejoining the others in 2035 if Lainey came for them. It would close the loop, and she would resume her role as the hamster on the wheel of the "prevent the apocalypse" team, possibly making 2035 as confining as 2075 had been. But here, in this new world she and Cyrus had stumbled upon, she could reshape her life in her own image; be the author of her own story for once in her damn life. The thought was somewhat terrifying since she'd been sheltered for so long, but it was also extremely liberating. Finally, she had a chance to experience what she'd only imagined: a fulfilling life, a passionate lover, and a family of her own.

Smirking at her desire for a lover, her thoughts drifted to Cyrus. Running her hand through her hair, she tried to calm the multitude of feelings swirling in her chest.

"You're both just trying to do your best," she murmured to herself, leaning back on her palms. "And he made the move, so he must be *somewhat* attracted to you even if he *was* high as a kite."

"You talking to yourself again, Finch?" his deep baritone chimed from above.

Grinning up at him, she said, "You know it."

"Well, I think it's time Montgomery and Finch began their mission. What do you say?"

Claire stared up, shielding her eyes from the sun as she squinted. "Our mission?"

"Well, we can't be 'π's for hire' if we don't have a case. Tell me what you found on Randolph, and let's get started."

The corner of her lip arched, and she understood what he was doing. It was easier to push aside their recent sexual encounter and concentrate on the task at hand than discuss it. Realizing he'd already buried it, Claire resigned herself to moving on. After all, it was pointless to focus on something he refused to even acknowledge.

Standing, she wiped her hands on her thighs as she grinned up at him. "He lives in Georgetown. We can take the bus and be there in less than thirty minutes. Are you going to be able to hobble along on the crutches, old man?"

He gave a "*pfft*" and waved a dismissive hand. "I'll run circles around you. Let's do it."

Stepping closer, she scrutinized him for any lingering signs of pain. "Are you sure you're okay, Cyrus? You've been through a lot. I don't want to run your body down again."

"I feel so much better today, and, honestly, I can't lie in that bed anymore. I need to do something productive. I think that's the best thing for me."

Craning her neck, she observed the air cast. "All right. You seem solid. Let's do it."

Half an hour later, they strode along the pristine sidewalk toward Edward Randolph's home. The neighborhood was so different from the one they were staying in, fully showcasing the inequities of the pre-apocalyptic world.

"It's amazing how there can be such economic disparity in neighborhoods within such close proximity," she said, shaking her head. "No wonder Randolph eventually seized power. The world isn't meant to function like this."

"It's definitely not sustainable. Hopefully, if Lainey resets the timeline, people will learn to live more cohesively. Otherwise, she might just be staving off one disaster that leads to another down the road."

"Let's hope not," Claire said as they approached Randolph's block. A large tree sat on the corner, and they slid behind it, still able to observe the home. A woman stepped onto the front porch and trailed down the stairs to the front walkway with a toddler on her hip. Approaching the end of the walkway, she bent to pick up the newspaper.

"Holy shit," Claire breathed. "I think that's Lewis."

Cyrus nodded. "Yep, and Lainey's grandmother, Alice. Lewis told me several stories about her."

"So freaking weird," she said, clutching the bark. "From what he told me, they weren't close."

"He said she was a cold woman who didn't show much tenderness. Both of his parents were enamored by the spotlight of politics and could never understand his more introverted, scientific personality. I get the feeling they weren't very affectionate."

"Perhaps that's why he was so affectionate with Mara and Lainey. He wanted to create something different than he'd experienced."

"That's definitely possible."

The woman headed back inside, and the house remained still.

Glancing up at Cyrus, Claire said, "Well, there doesn't seem to be much happening here. Should we try to track down Randolph at his office? It's about a five-minute bus ride."

"Sure."

Several minutes later, they stood on the sidewalk across from Edward Randolph's city council office. It sat on a busy street, and they waited for the walk signal before crossing. Cyrus was pretty adept at maneuvering on the crutches, and Claire admired his resilience. Breaching the sidewalk, they halted by the bus stop on the corner to gaze inside. There were many passersby on the busy thoroughfare, and Claire figured they blended in on the bustling street.

A man circulated inside, clean cut with a pristine blue tie over his white dress shirt, as he flitted between the desks full of people. He stopped at one desk, patting the young man on the back as he pointed to the document that sat atop the surface. Then, he approached another desk, smiling at the woman as she gazed up at him, asking a question. Edward nodded, and the woman gave a tilt of her head, turning back to resume her work.

"Seems like a pretty typical field office for a busy councilman," Claire said.

"Yep," Cyrus said, watchful as he stood beside her. "Who knew at this moment in time that the man inside would destroy the world?"

Shivering, Claire crossed her arms over her abdomen. "Heavy."

They observed for another minute before Edward exited the office. Lifting his face, the councilman inhaled the city air of the sunny early April day. Glancing around, he seemed to be looking for something...or perhaps he was just taking stock of people passing by. Lifting his cell phone from the case at his belt, he walked to the center of the block and disappeared into what looked to be an alleyway.

"Let's follow him," Claire said, curiosity threating to choke her. After all, they were now in the presence of the person who would one day become the most famous—and infamous—man in the world.

"Okay. Stay close to me," Cyrus's deep baritone directed.

Nodding, she began walking, telling herself to stay calm although her body was pulsing with anticipation. Approaching the alley, she maneuvered behind a large green dumpster, Cyrus close behind. Ears perked, she listened to Edward's deep voice as he grumbled into the phone.

"Goddammit!" he said, rubbing his forehead. "She'll jeopardize everything we've worked for. Sometimes, I think she does this shit just to spite me."

Silence laced the alleyway as he listened to the person on the other end of the call.

"She has childish notions of saving the damn world. I could never understand how someone so intelligent couldn't understand my vision. She was too stubborn to see things as they truly are—as we must fashion them to be. Infuriating woman," he muttered, harshly rubbing his fingers over his eyes. "I'll talk to her. Maybe I can sway her."

He gave a few more angry nods before clicking off the phone. Stuffing it in the case, he placed his hands on his hips, looked to the sky, and gave a loud sigh. Claire felt a tugging on her shirt and glanced up at Cyrus. His eyes held one message: *Time to go. Now.*

With a tilt of her head, she followed him toward the bright sunlight. Feeling the hairs on the back of her neck stand to attention, she turned, sparing one last glance toward Lainey's grandfather.

Fear bubbled in her throat as she stared back at the man who would one day give the order to decimate millions in a matter of seconds.

Breaking eye contact, she turned toward Cyrus. "Let's go. We'll walk a few blocks and catch the bus down the road."

Foreboding washed over her as they walked, Claire comprehending they'd most likely opened a can of worms that could have disastrous consequences for their safety.

* * * *

That night, Cyrus noted Claire's mood. She'd been like a dog with a bone since their encounter with Randolph, sending slight prickles of alarm up his spine. Although he agreed searching for intel on a young Edward could be helpful if Lainey came for them, he certainly didn't want to expose them to any danger. Randolph was already a powerful man with connected allies and resources, according to Claire's research, and inciting his ire wouldn't be smart. Especially for two people who had no connections or resources of their own.

Cyrus sat on the couch, elevating his leg, as Claire toiled on the internet in the soft chair next to him. As she researched Randolph's actions and associates, she became more entranced by the snippets of information she uncovered.

"He shut down three community centers in wards that bordered his because he felt they didn't promote the 'integrity' of Ward 2," she said, making quotation marks with her fingers. "What an ass. He's supposed to be a public servant."

"A rift between political ideals began to grow in the early twenty-first century," Cyrus said, lacing his fingers behind his head as he recalled the conversations he'd had about the pre-apocalyptic world with Lewis and Marie. "As wage and class disparity grew, the wealthy gained more power and wanted to keep it at all costs. Lewis told me Edward often spoke of his belief in one overarching government that willed the people into submission for their own good. He believed people's free will to make bad decisions led to their downfall and felt a systematic government would make better choices than individual citizens."

"But that goes against every democratic principle in the US constitution," she said, eyebrows drawing together.

Cyrus shrugged. "People often interpret things through their own lens. Lewis always seemed to have a reluctant respect for his father even though he disagreed with his actions. I think somewhere deep inside, he felt Edward was initially motivated by good intentions even though his exploits eventually turned disastrous."

Claire shook her head, staring absently at the glowing screen. Sighing, she clicked around the keyboard and shut the laptop. Rising, she set it on the coffee table and smiled down at Cyrus.

"How's the ankle feeling?"

"Good," he said, lifting his leg to assess the swelling. "The ibuprofen is working, I think."

"Good thing since you're done with the Percocet," she said, giving him a stiff smile.

Cyrus sensed her discomfort and wanted to put her at ease, especially since he was the one who'd crossed the line the previous evening. Claire was one of the only people he truly felt comfortable with, and he didn't want to lose their rapport.

Hoping to relieve the tension, he extended his hand. She took it, and he drew her to sit beside him.

"Are we okay? I'm so sorry, Claire. I feel terrible—"

"Can you do me a favor?" she interrupted, holding up a hand. "Can you stop apologizing for last night? It makes me feel worse. I understand you regret it—"

"I don't regret it," he said, squeezing her hand. "I just don't want to murk the waters. We need to focus on surviving here until Lainey hopefully comes for us, and I don't want to make the situation more tense. We're living in close proximity, and my primary goal is to protect you and help us navigate through this. Giving in to our attraction will complicate things on a scale I can't imagine."

Wide eyes searched his. "So, you're admitting you're attracted to me?" she asked, arching a brow as she bit her lip. Fuck, she was adorable.

"Yes," he said, his voice gravelly. "I think you're stunning, Claire. But you're still so young, and we're so different..." He trailed off, not wanting to hurt her feelings as he had that morning. He needed to urge her to let go of their attraction gently.

"Maybe our differences are what makes our relationship so awesome," she said, clenching his hand. "Who wants to be around people who are just like them? How freaking boring."

Chuckling, he nodded. "That would be pretty boring."

"Okay, we're cool. I've never felt weird around you and don't want to start now. We'll move on, but I do have to say, it was nice to get some action." She stood and wiped her hands on her thighs.

"I haven't had any action in a while either, so maybe we both needed it."

Her brow furrowed as she studied him.

"What?"

"I just..." Her shoulders lifted. "I saw Alora coming out of your room the night she returned. I thought you guys had..." She trailed off, gesturing with her hand.

"Nope," he said, shaking his head. "She brought me some supplies I'd requested. That was it."

"Oh," Claire said, blowing a breath past her bottom lip so it fanned the hair above her brow.

"Give me a sec," he said, grunting as he sat up. Claire reached down to help him, and he waved her off, determined to stand on his own. Grabbing the crutches, he ambled into the bedroom and searched through his bag. Locating the vials, he returned to stand before her.

"Green, blue, and orange," he said, the tiny bottles resting in his palm as his other hand clenched the crutch. "I knew you were running out of polish, so I asked Alora to get some for you. I was going to give it to you on your birthday in October." He gave her a sheepish smile. "I noticed you bought some at the drugstore the other day and figured you didn't really have a need for the crappy nail polish from 2075. The stuff in this timeline is much more vibrant."

Her throat bobbed as she reached for the vials, gently taking them from his hand. "Thank you, Cyrus. That's really thoughtful."

"You're welcome," he said, basking in her obvious joy. He adored seeing her smile, and knowing he was the cause of it spurred something tender in his pragmatic heart.

"You remember my birthday every year," she said softly. "It's really nice."

"You're so kind, Claire," he said, tucking a wayward strand of soft hair behind her ear. "I'll never be able to repay you for teaching me to read. The least I can do is remember your birthday."

"I can't wait to use these," she said, holding up the polish. "The orange is particularly stunning."

"I knew you'd like that one," he said, chest swelling with pride at her palpable elation.

"You're a good friend," she almost whispered, placing her palm over his pec, his heart pounding under his black T-shirt.

They stood like that for a moment, still and smiling, and Cyrus realized they were okay. Even if he'd fucked up the night before, they'd always be okay. They were Cyrus and Claire after all; two people who'd always had an unspoken understanding and affection between them.

"I can't wait to see it on you," he said, feeling his stomach growl through the tender moment. "But in the meantime, I think we should scrounge up some dinner."

"Ohhh," she said, eyes lighting up. "I can make us French toast if you want. I'm totally digging the unlimited bread in this timeline and am pretty sure I could eat French toast twenty-four-seven and never tire of it."

"Breakfast for dinner sounds great. I'm in."

Settling in, Cyrus ate the first of many French toast dinners Claire would eventually cook for him, enjoying every morsel almost as much as he relished her brilliant smile.

Chapter 11

"I want to check out the library," Claire said the next day, after they'd finished breakfast. "They should have archives of all the articles written on Randolph that I couldn't find online. What do you say?"

"All right," Cyrus said, anchoring to stand on the crutches. He was getting pretty damn tired of having to rely on them and couldn't wait to see Doc Viv for his appointment the next week. Hopefully, she'd tell him he could begin to put weight on his ankle again. "Let's do it."

Twenty minutes later, Cyrus stood enthralled by the multitude of shelves with endless books. Claire gazed up at him, her smile brilliant.

"Pretty cool, huh?"

"So damn cool," he said, pride circulating through his veins that he could now read most of the books in the massive facility.

"Don't think I'm going to let you slack," she teased. "Now that you've finished *Where the Red Fern Grows*, you've proven your skill. I expect you to help me slog through all the articles I dig up."

"Yes, ma'am," he said, giving her a good-natured salute. "Where do we start?"

They located a long mahogany table on the second floor that had plenty of seating and a computer at several of the stations. Claire sat in front of one of the monitors and began searching the archives. She located several articles on Randolph, and soon, they were studying them on the microfiche reader. Every so often, she'd send him to a particular location in the library that had printed articles, and he would return with the compilation of archives.

After several hours, she threw her pen atop the notebook that comprised the notes and rubbed her eyes. "Man, I'm beat. Slogging through old newspaper articles sucks."

"You're the one who wanted to become a P.I., Miss 'π for hire'," he said, arching an eyebrow.

Her features scrunched. "It seemed more fun in my head. Anyway," she said, flipping through the scribbled pages, "it looks like we found some good stuff. The two most important being the Knights of Washington and the alleged scandal in Randolph's past."

"The Knights of Washington seem to be a group of powerful men made up of local councilmen, senators, and members of congress," Cyrus said, gripping his chin as he thoughtfully stared at the notes. "They all have views that align with Randolph's. It's possible this is the precursor to the New Establishment."

"Definitely," she said, chewing her lip as she contemplated. "We could gather more intel on the members and compile it for Lainey if and when she comes for us."

"And what about the scandal? There's far less information on that."

"It was mostly relegated to the gossip and society sections, but the reporting was solid. President Randolph had an affair that ended badly while he was engaged to Alice. I wonder if the woman is still in D.C. She was only mentioned as the 'alleged other woman.'"

"Worth a shot trying to locate her. Affairs of the heart can create a powerful connection. Perhaps she still has some sway over him. That could come in handy down the road."

Claire's smile made his pulse quicken.

"What?"

"What do you know about affairs of the heart?" she asked softly.

Breathing a laugh, he shook his head. "Not much, that's for damn sure. So what's next?"

"We need to reshelve all the archives, and I'd like to find a few books to check out. I can find a new one for you to read too. I should be able to get a library card with my fake ID."

"I'm ready for a new book, and for a new word of the day. You haven't given me one of those in a while."

"You're right," she said, glancing toward the ceiling, one eye squinted. "I need to think of a good one."

"Go on and browse the bookshelves," he said, gesturing with his head. "I'll reshelve everything."

"You're a prince," she said, standing and stretching her arms above her head, the fabric of her V-neck T-shirt straining over those glorious breasts. "Especially because you're on crutches. Meet me downstairs at the front desk in twenty?"

"Aye, aye, captain," he said. She trailed off, the globes of her ass filing every inch of her tight blue jeans, and Cyrus's body hardened. "Shut it down, man," he muttered.

It took him a while with his still-swollen ankle, but he managed to return the archives to their rightful places. Glancing around, he saw Claire between the shelves, deep in conversation with a young man. His demeanor was unassuming, his smile broad as he nodded at something she said. Not sure if he was a threat, Cyrus decided to sit at the nearby table and keep an eye on them. A moment before he turned to move, he caught someone else out of the corner of his eye.

Inconspicuous and dressed in black, a man with dark hair and broad shoulders sat at the end of one of the long wooden tables. A book rested in his hands, open in front of his face, but it was obvious to Cyrus he wasn't looking at the pages. The man was watching Claire.

Adrenaline surged through his frame, and the instinct to protect her closed his throat. Moving with measured speed on the crutches, he headed toward her.

"We need to go," he said, interrupting her conversation with the man she'd befriended.

"I, uh, Fred...this is Cyrus. He's unspeakably rude," she said, shooting him a questioning glare. "What the hell?"

"Fred Savage," the man said with a slight accent, extending his hand. Cyrus couldn't quite place the accent, but if he had to guess, he'd wager Australian. "No relation to the actor, although it does lead to some confusion sometimes." He smiled, kindness in his light eyes behind black-rimmed glasses.

"Pleasure," he said, briefly shaking the man's hand. "Claire, it's time to go."

"Wow," Fred said, wringing his hand through the air a few times. "You've got a mean shake there, man."

"What's going on?" Claire whispered loudly, reminding them they were still in a library.

Cyrus glanced between the books to notice the man in black had disappeared. Locking his gaze on Fred, he gave him a silent directive to beat it.

"Well, um, it was nice to meet you, Cyrus, and really nice to meet you, Claire." His cheeks flushed under his pale skin. "See you around." With a wave, he sauntered through the bookshelves, out of sight.

"Do you want to tell me why you're acting like a crazy person?" she asked, hands fisted on her hips.

"Did Fred approach you?"

"I was reading the blurb of a book, and when I looked up, he was scouring the shelf to my left. We made eye contact, he seemed nice, and we struck up a conversation."

"And that doesn't seem odd to you? A random man striking up a conversation with a complete stranger?"

"I was just being cordial." She shrugged. "We met so few people at the hub, it was cool to chat with someone new, even if it was just a short conversation. People can be nice just for the heck of it, you know?"

"Not likely." His lips drew into a firm line. "Someone was watching you from that table over there. It was suspicious. I don't think it's safe here."

Concern washed over her face. "It might have to do with what happened yesterday."

Cyrus's nostrils flared. "What happened yesterday?"

Her throat bobbed as she swallowed. "Don't be mad, okay?" she asked, a plea in those wide green eyes.

If there was one thing Cyrus had learned, nothing good ever resulted from those words when uttered from Claire's lips. Like the time she'd said them before she dragged him outside to show him the rubble that had once been Marie's shed. Claire had gotten it in her head that she wanted to play around with some of the chemicals Zach had created in his makeshift lab to try to create longer-lasting hair dye. Instead, she'd set Marie's shed on fire, and the woman had been spitting mad. It had taken Cyrus several weeks to rebuild the little shack to the exact specifications the surly woman would accept without complaint.

There was also the time she'd uttered them before showing him Lewis's broken fishing pole. It had been his favorite, and Claire had accidentally tripped over it, snapping it in half. Cyrus had toiled the entire night in Marie's shed, but he'd eventually repaired the damn thing.

Or when she'd grabbed his wrist and led him to the large oak tree that sat several yards into the woods surrounding the hub. She'd lowered to the ground and stroked the tiny puppies as they squirmed. "I told them we'd take care of them," she'd said, staring up at him from her crouched position. "Lainey will freak, but I can't break my promise to them, Cyrus."

"We can't have two puppies at the hub, Claire," he'd said, attempting to be firm but compassionate. "They'll grow into dogs, and dogs bark. They'll make too much noise."

Undeterred, she'd proceeded to make her case until Cyrus realized something very important: he didn't possess the ability to say no to Claire. Never had, and never would. They'd carried the two pups back to the hub, and they'd both lived wonderful lives for their respective seven and nine years on the planet.

And now, here they were, those dreaded but meaningful words hanging between them again. Feeling himself scowl, Cyrus asked, "Don't be mad at what?"

Inhaling deeply, she lifted her chin. "Randolph saw us watching him in the alley yesterday."

* * * *

Claire sat beside Cyrus on the bus consumed by the waves of frustration and concern emanating from his stiff shoulders. Man, he was pissed. It made sense, of course. She should have told him about the ominous glare of recognition she'd seen from Randolph in the alleyway. Questioning why she hadn't, she sighed and contemplated the answer.

When they exited the bus, she lifted her hand to help him down the stairs, but he just shot her a glare and maneuvered the crutches under his arms. Silently, they headed to the apartment as she worried he might not forgive her. Lord knew, she'd fucked up in the past, and he'd always let it go. Would this time be different?

Once inside, she locked the door behind them as Cyrus trailed to the center of the room. Standing in front of the couch, he tossed the crutches to the floor and faced her, hands wide on his hips as smoke threatened to simmer from his bald head.

"What do you mean, Randolph saw us yesterday?" he asked, a muscle ticking in his jaw.

"When we were leaving," she said, lifting her hands in an aimless shrug, "I turned and looked back. He glared at me and left no doubt he saw me."

Cyrus's eyebrows lifted. "And you're only telling me this now because...?"

"I don't know," she said, unable to explain why she'd kept it from him. Searching deep inside, she circled her hand as she reached for words. "I wasn't sure if it was a big deal. I mean, who are we to him anyway? He's a public figure. I'm sure people watch him all the time."

"A public figure who's capable of mass murder and has powerful connections!" Claire jolted at the force of his tone. "Damn it, Claire, you can't keep stuff like this from me. I need to know everything. I'm the only protection you have—for now at least."

Tears stung her eyes, and she told herself not to be a damn baby. She'd brought this on herself. Realizing how stupid—and how dangerous—it was not to tell him, she ran her teeth over her bottom lip in a nervous gesture.

"I'm sorry—"

"Sorry doesn't cut it this time," he said, slicing a hand through the air. "From now on, I want to know everything. If your shoe comes untied, I want to know, Claire. Do you hear me?"

She nodded, lips curling inward, as she struggled to hold back the tears. "I promise," she whispered.

Silence spread between them, so heavy it threatened to choke her, and she wanted to melt into the floor. Cyrus rarely showed emotion. The fact he was livid meant she'd really fucked up, big-time. Unable to look at the disappointment in his eyes, she closed her own, furious at herself.

Hearing his ragged breath, her shoulders stiffened as he hobbled closer. Warm hands bracketed her face, tilting it. Lifting her lids, she stared into his eyes.

"We're a team, Claire. That's why I'm so pissed. I would never recover if anything happened to you, and I can only keep you safe if we communicate."

"I know," she said, mortified at the lone tear that trailed down her cheek. "It won't happen again. I didn't want to amplify something that wasn't important."

"Damn it, Finch," he said, wiping the tear with his thumb. "Now I feel like a piece of shit. Why are you crying?"

"Because I let you down."

"Sweetheart," he whispered, shaking his head. "*I* let *you* down. Because I didn't realize he'd spotted us. That's why I'm so upset. I'm disabled here and not able to see everything I should," he said, jerking his head toward his ankle. "So I need your help. That's all. Please don't cry."

"You know I'm a sap," she said, shrugging. "Asking me not to cry is like asking a black cloud not to rain. It's kind of pointless."

His warm chuckle caressed her skin, and she released a ragged, relieved exhale. Standing here, with his calloused palms against her cheeks, she knew he'd already forgiven her. "It is, but let's dry the tears anyway. I'm sorry I yelled at you."

"I know. I'm sorry I fucked up. I'll tell you everything from now on, like whether it's a number one or a number two on my way to the john."

His face contorted. "Gross, Finch. I need you take it down to ninety-nine percent. Not a hundred. Ninety-nine will do."

Laughing, she nodded. "Got it."

"Come on," he said, lowering his hands and encircling her wrist to draw her beside him on the couch. "Tell me everything. Exactly what you remember from when he spotted you yesterday. And then I need to write down everything I remember about the man in black I saw in the library."

Nodding, they got to work detailing everything from the two short encounters so they could be armed with as much shared information as possible.

Chapter 12

The next day, they returned to the library. Claire wanted to do more research, and Cyrus refused to let her go alone. It was honestly quite adorable, and she realized messing up might have inadvertently created a situation in which he was glued to her side. She could live with that. Having a super-hot soldier intent on guarding you was pretty damn awesome after all.

As she waded through stacks of newspaper articles in the archive section, she felt a presence next to her. Glancing up, she was met with a blinding smile.

"Caramel macchiato," a smooth voice said, handing her a paper cup. "I took a guess it would be your favorite."

"Hi, Fred," she said, smiling at the man she'd met yesterday. "What's a caramel macchiato? Is it like coffee?"

"So much better," he said, thrusting the cup at her. "Give it a try."

Taking it, she glanced over at Cyrus, who was reading at the nearby mahogany table. She'd recommended *A Wrinkle in Time* as his next read, and he seemed enthralled by the story. Still, Claire knew the experienced fighter was aware of her current conversation. Although his eyes were fixed on the page, his shoulders were set, and his body was alert. Every tiny hair on her skin prickled, both in gratitude and comfort that he was protecting her.

"Not to sound like an ass, but I don't really drink concoctions from strangers," she said, eyeing the drink. "Cyrus over there is former military, and he'll probably remove all your extremities if this is poisoned."

"Um, wow," Fred said, visibly swallowing as he glanced at Cyrus. "I swear, it came straight from Starbucks to you. There was another girl named Claire getting a latte, so I had them write something different on your order."

Lifting the cup, Claire examined the scrawl. *Pretty Girl in the Library.* Aw. That was kind of cute, actually. And maybe a bit creepy. Eyes narrowed, she asked, "How did you know I would be here?"

"I came in early this morning and saw you two arrive. I needed coffee anyway, so I figured I'd get you something as well. Sorry. Maybe it was a bad idea."

Claire studied him, a bit sheepish but quite attractive with his shaggy brown hair and wire-rimmed glasses. Feeling safe since Cyrus was nearby, she took a tentative sip of the drink. It tasted like heaven.

"Yum," she said, closing her eyes. "It's fantastic. Thank you."

"You're welcome," he said, smiling. His gaze trailed to her stacks of newspapers. "What are you researching?"

"Oh, nothing you'd find interesting," she said, waving her hand. Although he seemed nice, Claire had learned long ago to be wary, and she wasn't going to share any of her intel on Randolph with anyone but Cyrus. "Politics and old society pages. I could use a break though. Want to sit over there and chat for a few? Quietly, of course. I'm new to D.C. and would love to pick your brain."

"Sure."

They sat in the two leather chairs at the end of a row of bookshelves, Claire feeling Cyrus's gaze on her the entire time. By the time her macchiato was finished, she'd learned Fred was an eleventh-grade physics and chemistry teacher who'd lived in D.C. since moving from Australia with his family at twelve years old. He was currently on spring break and enjoyed hanging in the library during his time off. He recommended several parks, local restaurants, and museums to her, and Claire was taken by his kindness.

"Thanks so much for letting me grill you," she said, standing and tossing her cup in the nearby trash can. "I can't wait to try some of the places you recommended. Unfortunately, I've got to get back to work."

"Sorry I didn't give you much time to talk," he said, blushing. "Are you a society reporter or something? Is that why you're searching the articles?"

"Oh, um, yeah. I guess you could say that." Searching for something that would be a plausible excuse, she said, "I'm looking to start my own blog. Gossip, society, local politics, that sort of thing. Want to make sure I research properly." Blogs were a thing in 2002, right? Hoping like hell they were, she waited for his response.

"Well, good luck with it. I'll leave you to it. Hope it turns out to be really successful for you."

"Thanks, Fred." Relief washed over her that the story seemed plausible. "Hopefully, I'll see you here again soon."

His hazel eyes searched hers. "I mean, you could give me your phone number. If that's not weird or anything. I'd love to see you outside the library."

"Oh, um." Claire stuck her hands in the back pockets of her jeans, chewing her bottom lip as she wondered what to do. "I, uh, well...I think Cyrus and I want to keep that number private."

"Oh," he said, brow forming a frown. "Are you two...together?"

Claire breathed a laugh and ran a hand through her hair. "It's kind of complicated," she said. That was honest, at least.

"Got it. Well, let me at least give you my number," he said, holding out his hand. "I can program it in your phone."

Claire pondered for a moment and decided that wouldn't hurt. Handing him the phone, he typed in his name and number and saved it in her contacts.

"You don't have a lot of contacts in your phone," he said, handing it back to her as his eyebrows drew together.

"Like I said, I'm new here and just got this puppy." She shook the phone before placing it back in her pocket. "As I meet people, I'm sure I'll fill it up. Thanks for the macchiato, Fred. It was really good."

Realizing he'd been dismissed, he gave her a brief salute. "Bye, Claire. Please call anytime. Take care."

Once he was out of sight, Claire moseyed over to Cyrus. "How's the book?"

"Good," he muttered, closing it before placing his broad hand over it. "How's Fred?"

"Good," she said, unable to read his mood. "He got me a caramel macchiato. It's probably loaded with sugar that will go straight to my hips, but it was fantastic."

His eyes darted toward her hips, assessing before his gaze lifted back to hers. God, the way this man looked at her sometimes... It was disconcerting and confusing, both at once. Circling her hand over her face, she said, "You're doing it again. That weird look thing."

"Sorry." Standing, he picked up the book and held it to his chest. "Can we check this out? I want to keep reading it."

"Sure," she said, taking the book so he could place the crutches under his arms. "I need to get a library card anyway since I didn't get one yesterday. Let's go to the front desk."

Once she'd secured the library card using the fake ID Zach had created, they headed back home. After Cyrus was situated on the couch, ankle elevated, they got to work cataloging the information Claire had jotted in her notebook.

"We still have no idea who Randolph had an affair with," Claire said from the kitchen as she made sandwiches for dinner. "But we've definitely uncovered most of his associates. His web of powerful and mysterious people is vast."

"Yes," Cyrus said, taking the plate she handed him when she stopped beside the couch. Lowering to the floor, she took a huge bite, smiling as she chewed up at him. "We can do some reconnaissance on his associates but only in public places where we'll blend in. I don't want to put you in any further danger."

"Aye, aye, chief," she said, saluting with her sandwich. "The surveillance part of this whole P.I. business is my favorite. I don't really like the research part."

"I think it comes with the territory." The muscles in his jaw worked as he chewed a bite. Swallowing, he said, "Claire, we can't stall forever. There's a very real possibility Lainey isn't coming for us. We need to start preparing ourselves for that."

She nodded thoughtfully. "I know. The thought of starting over here, all by ourselves, is so daunting. It's easier to cling to what we know."

"But it might be futile. I think we need to agree on a hard date where we'll give up on the notion she's coming for us. It doesn't have to be tomorrow, but we need a plan for the rest of our lives if we're stuck here."

Claire's eyes darted between his. "What would you want to do? In this new life?"

"I don't know," he said, eyebrows drawing together. "The most important thing would be to get you set and make sure you're safe, and then I could probably find some sort of security job."

"And how would you ensure I'm set?"

"Make sure you have a job, somewhere you can put that brilliant brain to use, and ensure you're set up to find a good man and make a family. Fred seems nice." Was he scowling as he said the words? Claire couldn't quite tell.

"He is. He told me I'm pretty."

"You are." The words were grunted as he slightly tilted his head.

Inwardly sighing, Claire realized that was all she was getting out of the impassive man. Rising, she stacked his empty plate over hers and walked to the sink.

"I want to use the bathroom before we get you set up in bed, if you don't mind. I bought a hair dye kit at the drugstore with this kick-ass blue color. Can't wait to try hair dye that I didn't have to make myself. I think the chemicals are supposed to be bad for you, but I say bring it on."

"You can start sleeping in the bed, Claire. I feel terrible I've taken it for this long. I can sleep on the couch."

"No way," she said, observing his frame on the too-small couch. "Your ankle will heal better in the bed. That couch is hella uncomfortable."

"Which is why I want you to sleep on the bed."

"Nope," she said, striding to the coffee table and picking up *A Wrinkle in Time*. Handing it to him, she asked, "How close are you to finishing?"

"About halfway."

"Read up. There will be a quiz later from your newly dyed teacher. I'll leave the door cracked. Call for me if you need anything."

Grabbing the plastic bag by the door, she zipped to the bathroom, excited to spruce up her hair.

Chapter 13

"Cyrus!"

The scream ricocheted through his frame, causing him to jolt on the couch. As the forgotten book fell to the floor, Cyrus grabbed the crutches and hauled ass toward the bathroom.

"What's wrong?" he asked, breathless as he pushed open the door.

Claire stood by the sink clad in only her bra and panties, her hair under some sort of cap as tiny strands extended through the plastic.

"Oh, god," she moaned, her face a thousand shades of red. "As embarrassed as I am for you to see me this way, I need your help. I didn't realize this dye kit was for highlights. I'm supposed to use the hook thingy to pull the hair through, but I dropped it in the sink. I can't get the damn thing out."

Stepping closer, careful not to touch her exposed skin—and trying even harder not to stare—Cyrus craned his neck. A tiny plastic stick was stuck in the drain. Reaching down, he latched on and tugged. After a few seconds, it popped free.

"Thank goodness," she said, taking it from him. "I was already having enough trouble hooking the hair in back. You saved me."

Cyrus should've probably smiled to help ease her embarrassment, but he was having all sorts of trouble talking at the moment. Or breathing. Or thinking, for that matter. Claire, in all her luscious curves and natural beauty, stood before him practically naked. It didn't matter that she looked ridiculous with the tiny strands of hair pulled through the cap atop her head. Not to his body, and definitely not to his dick, which was rapidly jerking to attention inside his pants.

"Sorry," she rasped, giving him that curious look he'd come to know. "This must seem so stupid to you."

Cyrus licked his suddenly parched lips. "Do you want me to do the back?" he almost growled.

Her eyebrows drew together. "What?" she whispered.

"You said you'd have a hard time hooking the hair on the back of your head. Do you want me to do it?"

"Oh, I..." Her throat bobbed as she swallowed. "It might take a few minutes. I don't want to stress your ankle."

"Give me the hook," he said, taking it from her hands. Hopping behind her since he'd set the crutches against the wall, he gently slid his hands over the smooth skin of her shoulders. Straightening her to face the mirror, his gaze locked with hers in the reflection. "How do I do it?"

Her eyes widened, perhaps at the slight double entendre or maybe because her breath was now as labored as his. "Just stick the hook in and turn it, then pull the strand out."

Nodding, he got to work. The plastic cap had small black circles that directed him where to insert and pull. With each released strand, he assessed her in the mirror, encouraged by her tiny nods that he was performing the task correctly.

Air, heavy and thick, permeated the cramped bathroom as he worked. Somewhere along the way, her body inched toward his until her ass was curved into the juncture of his thighs, her back against his abdomen. Her head was bent so he could access her lower scalp, and he imagined having her just like this as he took her from behind.

His fingers would clench her thick, vibrant-colored hair, causing the slightest bit of decadent pain as he rammed his cock inside her deepest place. His other hand would latch onto that glorious ass, squeezing the flesh until it was red, marking her as *his*. Unable to suppress the dirty thoughts, he ground his now near-to-bursting cock against her, not even realizing he'd made the evocative gesture until she pushed back against him.

"Cyrus," she whispered, eyes closed as her head tilted forward. The submissive position caused him to grit his teeth, and he refocused on the task at hand before he made another stupid mistake—one that couldn't be blamed on pain medication since he was sober as a choir girl.

"Shh..." he said, as much to himself as her, wanting to quiet the arousal humming through his body. "I'm almost done."

The little minx straightened her spine, stretching her body, and he squeezed the juncture of her neck and shoulder. "Be still, okay?"

"Yes, sir," she teased, the words igniting a possessive firestorm inside his body. God, what he wouldn't give to hear those words as she kneeled before him, hands tied behind her back as she awaited further instruction. *Goddammit.* Inhaling a shaky breath, he proceeded to finish his task.

"I think that's all of them," he said, placing the hook on the sink counter. "You should be good to go."

Her gaze locked with his in the mirror. "Thank you," she said, body still flush against his.

Damning himself to hell, he realized he didn't have the willpower to move without tasting her. He'd fantasized about kissing Claire on those full pink lips for so long, the desire was choking him. Cupping her jaw, he gently tilted her face to his.

"Once, Claire," he said into those swimming green eyes. "So I can finally stop wondering. After that, no more."

"Once is a good start," she said, his body tightening at her silken tone. "But I can't promise I won't want more—"

Done with words, he devoured her lips, covering them with his own and plunging his tongue inside her wet mouth.

* * * *

Claire's groan began somewhere deep in her gut, near the place where butterflies of arousal and anxiety were turning her inside out. Encircling Cyrus's neck with her arm, she vaguely remembered she looked like a complete idiot under the silly hair cap. Who cared when his silken tongue was invading her mouth, sweeping and wet as she struggled to stand?

His low growl vibrated through her as his tongue brushed over hers, spurring a gush of wetness between her thighs. Searching for a stronghold, she slid her other arm down his waist, grabbing onto his ass and drawing him close. Their position was awkward, his body bracketing her back and side, but Claire didn't give a damn. The little nub between her now slick folds pulsed each time her ragged heartbeat pushed blood through her veins. Desperate to soothe the ache, she whimpered, spearing her nails into his neck.

The action was rewarded with a tightening of Cyrus's body as he groaned. The sound was melodious...like nothing she'd ever heard, deep and full of yearning. Hoping to stoke his desire, even though she wasn't nearly as experienced as he, she worked her tongue against his. Sliding...stroking...sucking him between her lips as she milked him, suddenly dying to drop to her knees and take a different part of his body into her mouth...

67

"Damn it," he whispered, his body shuddering as his arms tightened around her. Resting his forehead against hers, he stared into her eyes, softly panting. "You taste so fucking good, Finch."

Since the ability to form words was long forgotten by her quivering body, she reached for his hand and encircled his wrist. Slowly trailing it down her body, her skin trembled beneath each tiny patch of skin his fingers touched. Sliding his hand under the waistband of her panties, she guided him toward her center, dripping and wet. The boldness was potent and strange, yet empowering and freeing, as she gazed into his hooded eyes. She'd never closed herself off from Cyrus, so perhaps that was why she dared to ask him for more. Who better to trust than the man she cherished with all her heart? Releasing every fear and doubt, she commanded, "Touch me."

His struggle was evident, from the intensity of his gaze to the firm set of his wet lips doused with her saliva. The sight caused something primal to well within. Pushing his fingers between her folds, she sighed.

"Cyrus—"

The word ended on a gasp as his fingers burrowed between the swollen flesh, sliding down her wet slit toward her opening. Circling it, he gathered some of the moisture and trailed it back up to her clit. Supporting her head with his other hand, he began to circle. "Is that what you want, sweetheart?" he murmured, nipping her bottom lip before sucking it between his teeth. As his teeth and tongue worked magic on her lip, his hand delivered the perfect pressure to her straining nub.

"Oh, god," she breathed, eyes closing as her head fell limp. Never did she question whether he would support her. Solid against her, he was her guidepost in this moment as he'd been in so many others. Succumbing to the pleasure, she relaxed, every nerve in her body open and willing.

"I need to know how tight you are," he said, his tone silken as he slid his finger back to her opening. Breath mingling with hers, he pushed his finger inside her wet channel.

"Yesss," he hissed, inching forward, stretching her, before drawing back only to push inside again. "Like a sweet little vise. Does that feel good?"

"*Mnhmnhnnn...*" was her incoherent reply.

A laugh escaped his lips, warm against her chin, as he nuzzled her face. "I've rendered you speechless. Never thought I'd see the day."

Through with any attempt at conversation, she pushed into his hand, needing more, reaching for something.

"I've got you," he said, gliding his soaked finger back up to her nub. "Pull yourself open for me."

Her hand shot to her core, separating the folds to expose her pulsing clit. The pads of his fingers circled her, sending sparks of intense pleasure to every vibrating cell in her body. Whimpers lodged in her throat as the heat intensified, spreading through her frame until she thought she might combust. Resting his lips against the shell of her ear, Cyrus spoke the words that set her free.

"Come all over me, honey."

Lightning surged up her spine as the orgasm hit, blinding her although her eyes were already closed. Shuddering for dear life, she gave herself over to the remarkable sensation. Sparks of pleasure ignited along infinite points of skin—tiny fireworks that threatened to drown her in sated lust. Cyrus's arms were so firm beneath her, holding her steady, as her body quaked and shuddered. Inhaling huge gulps of air, she struggled to regain coherence.

"It's okay, sweetheart," he murmured into her ear, causing her limp body to quiver yet again. "You look so pretty right now."

The chuckle began deep in her throat, spreading until it became a full-on laugh. As the joyful sound enveloped them, she attempted to open her eyes although the effort was futile.

"I look like a freaking idiot. Stupid cap and my hair..." She absently waved her hand through the air, then dropped her arm. The gesture required too much energy for her depleted body. Snuggling into his warmth, she smiled behind her closed lids. "Just need a minute, chief. Sorry. Can't function."

The deep rumble of his laughter vibrated against her side. Placing a tender kiss to her temple, he waited for her to recover. After what felt like a million years, she lifted her lids to find him grinning at her.

"Thanks for helping with my hair."

"Welcome," he mumbled, helping her to balance on her own two feet. Feeling wobbly, she grabbed the sink.

"Whoa," he said, hands gripping her waist. "Careful."

Biting her lip, she stared at him in the reflection. "If we get this worked up when I look like this,"—she pointed to her head—"imagine how hot we'd be if I looked anywhere near normal."

Chuckling, he gave her a good-natured wink. "Don't ever look normal, Finch. I like you just the way you are."

Aw. Her heart expanded so broadly at the words she thought it might jump from her chest. "Thank you," she almost whispered.

He squeezed her shoulder. "I'm going to let you finish here unless you need me to do something else to help you. That was a lot of action for my ankle. I need to sit down."

"Crap," she said, giving the ankle a glance. "Are you okay? Sorry. I totally forgot."

"It's fine," he said, extricating himself from her touch. Claire felt the loss immediately. "I'll be in the living room." He grabbed the crutches and placed them under his arms.

"Don't you want me to, um...well, I don't want to leave you hanging."

Glancing over his shoulder, he smiled. "I'm good. Excited to see how the highlights turn out." Pivoting, he trudged from the bathroom.

"Well, *that* was interesting," Claire muttered to herself, wondering how in the hell she was going to mix the dye while her hands were furiously shaking. Man, that had been *intense.* Cyrus could delude himself all he wanted, but their chemistry was flammable. Thanking the universe that he seemed to vehemently desire her, she began mixing the concoction to turn her hair blue. Only time would tell if they could figure out a way to turn their mutual desire into a romantic relationship. Although she craved that with every fiber of her still-pulsing body, Cyrus seemed intent on fighting it.

Arching an eyebrow, she gazed at herself in the reflection as she began applying the dye to her hair. Yes, her sexy soldier was stubborn as hell. Good thing she was pretty damn tenacious herself. Determined to win him over, she vowed to dedicate herself to showing Cyrus she could be everything he needed. Lover. Confidant. Partner. Claire was determined to use her fastidious brain to figure out how to build a future with him. Her heart would accept nothing less.

* * * *

Cyrus sat on the couch absently staring at his elevated ankle as he pondered. At this point, he was beyond beating himself up. He'd done that last time he lost control with Claire. This time, there were no excuses. He'd had every opportunity to let her go, but the sentiment was as futile as chopping off his own arm.

Accepting reality was one of his greatest strengths, and there, in the dim light of the couch-side lamp, Cyrus accepted the reality he must end their cohabitation. The thought burned since his greatest desire was to keep her safe, but he now felt that mission was compromised by his unchecked attraction to her.

"You just couldn't let her go, man," he muttered to himself, running a frustrated hand over his face. Sighing, the minutes ticked by as he strategized how to move forward. Somewhere along the way, the pipes creaked, and he knew Claire was washing the dye from her hair. Eventually, the hair dryer sounded, and a moment later, she walked out looking refreshed and so very young.

"So what do you think?" she asked, pointing at her multicolored hair. "Do I look ridiculous?"

Blue streaks intertwined with violet, falling slightly past her shoulders in a thick wave. It should've looked absurd. Instead, his heart slammed in his chest as he took in the luscious strands surrounding her flushed cheeks and bright smile.

"You look stunning," he said truthfully.

Biting her lip, she stuck her hands in her pockets. Bare feet peeked out below her jeans, the nails painted with the orange color he'd given her. She looked extremely nervous, and he wanted to squelch the awkwardness between them before it grew any worse.

"Come sit down," he said, shifting his ankle so his legs stretched out before him. Once she was beside him, he took her hand.

"Crap," she said, gnawing her lip. "I don't have a good feeling about this."

He gently laced his fingers through hers. "I won't apologize for touching you. For kissing you. It's something I've wanted to do for a very long time."

"You have?" she asked, excitement glowing in her eyes.

"Yes," he said, nodding. "But this can't go on, Claire. Entering into a sexual relationship isn't a good idea for a ton of reasons."

Extreme disappointment clouded her features as they drew together. "I don't think that's true—"

"It is," he said, clenching her hand as he interrupted her. "I'm well into my forties and have no idea if I even want to contemplate having kids at this age. Our visions for the future are quite different. Plus, our age gap is significant. There are other obstacles too. I just don't think you want to acknowledge them."

A muscle ticked in her jaw as anger flashed in her eyes. "Why are you so dead set against even trying?"

"This is a terrible time to start a romantic relationship, Claire. We're stranded in a different timeline and have a ton of other priorities we need to focus on."

Her eyes narrowed. "*You* kissed *me* in the bathroom—and in your bed, if I remember correctly. I'm not the one making moves here, chief."

"I know." Blowing a breath through puffed cheeks, he shook his head. "Thanks for the reminder. I seem to have a problem keeping my hands to myself around you, Finch. You're pretty damn irresistible, in case you haven't noticed."

"Then don't push me away," she said, scooting closer, her thigh brushing his. "Let's try to build something together. Don't we at least owe ourselves that opportunity?"

"No," he said, disentangling his hand from hers. "We need to begin establishing separate lives, Claire. It sucks because I need to keep you safe, but we can't continue living together. It's distracting and compromising my ability to protect you."

Hating that tears sparkled in her eyes, he waited for her to speak. "You'd just leave me? In a timeline where I have no one but you?"

"No way," he said, annoyed she would even think he'd desert her. "I think I should rent a separate room from Paul, here in the house. I can still protect you, but we can begin to build our own lives. I'll work with you to track down info on Randolph, but we should also plant the seeds of a new life here, Claire. Get jobs. Meet new people. We have to accept Lainey might never come for us."

"So we have one epic make out session, and you're writing me off forever? That's pretty shitty, Cyrus."

He glanced toward the ceiling, reminding himself to stay calm. Claire was emotional and had a mean temper. He'd seen her go off more than once at the hub, although she'd never unleashed her fury on him. Determined to keep it that way, he faced her and kept his tone even.

"I'm doing what's best for both of us, Claire. This situation isn't constructive for either of us."

"You listen to me right now, Cyrus Montgomery," she said, standing and pointing a finger in his face. "I won't sit idly by and let you tell me

what's right and wrong for my life. Those are *my* choices, damn it!"
Stomping her foot, she glared down at him, gorgeous and fierce. "You
think you can strongarm me because you're 'older and wiser,'"—she made
quotation marks with her fingers—"or whatever the hell you've made up
in your mind, but let me tell you something, mister." Leaning down, she
poked his pec several times. "I'm ready to fight for what I want in my life.
To fight for *us*."

"It takes more than desire and friendship to build a successful
relationship, Claire. I know you understand this deep inside."

"Oh, posh!" Slicing a hand through the air, it landed on her hip. "You
know what? I *am* taking the bed tonight. Stay out here and struggle on the
damn couch and take some time to consider what you really want. If
there's one thing we both should've learned by now, it's that life is too
short to squander a connection like ours. We both feel it, and we've been
dancing around this for a while now."

Bending at the waist, she glowered at him. "I was never sure if you felt
attraction toward me or just friendship, but now that I know you want me
back, I'm not letting you push me away, Cyrus. I'm so damn tired of
denying myself and letting other people decide what's best. It's time I take
control of my own life, and I'm determined for that life to include you."
Chin held high, she gave him a dismissive nod, pivoted, and marched to the
bedroom, slamming the door behind her.

Holy hell. Resting his face in his hand, Cyrus reflected on how badly the
discussion had devolved. Sighing, he decided he'd let her stew while he
figured out how the hell to fix what he'd broken.

Chapter 14

After a restless night of sleep, Cyrus rolled his head, attempting to loosen his aching neck muscles. The resounding pops and cracks reminded him that he was indeed on the wrong side of forty. Standing, he stretched, testing his ankle. He was able to put some weight on it without excruciating pain, and the swelling was much better. At least one thing was going right in his life.

Lips drawn into a firm line, he decided it would be best to confront Claire now, before their argument festered and the resentment grew. Remembering her angry passion spurred a smile as he ambled to the bedroom door. Man, she was fierce. He'd never been scolded so eloquently even by Marie, who was a master. Even in her fury, Claire had been amazing, vowing to fight for him; for *them*. Unfortunately, it wasn't in the cards for them. They were too different, and their age difference was significant. Understanding she'd eventually realize this as well, he knocked on the door.

"Claire?"

The resulting silence incited an eye roll. Pouting would get them nowhere, although he appreciated her stubbornness.

"Come on, Claire—"

Stopping short, Cyrus assessed the bed. It was freshly made and empty. Glancing around, he noticed the note on the bedside table.

At the library. You were sleeping, so I decided to go alone. I'm still mad, but I might forgive you. Bringing me one of those delicious caramel macchiatos might help. See you there. C

Grinning, he held the scrap of paper to his chest knowing she'd already forgiven him. Still, he'd get her the damn drink, if only because it would result in one of her beaming, crooked smiles. Excited at the thought, he prepped for the day, ready to set things right.

* * * *

Claire jumped when the low-toned voice spoke in her ear. "Got you a latte today," Fred said, sliding it in front of her and shaking it. "I think you'll like this one too."

"Fred," she said, shaky as she forced a smile. He grinned back, unassuming, but something felt...*off*. Coincidence was one thing, but he seemed to be searching her out, and that set off tiny bells of warning in her head. "Thank you." Grasping the cup, she lifted it in a salute and mimicked drinking, although she didn't imbibe any of the liquid. "Yum," she said, the word falsely cheerful.

He proceeded to converse with her in the back corner of the library, behind the shelves. It was rather secluded, and she began to feel unsafe. Gathering the newspapers she'd been cataloguing, she stacked them and stood.

"Well, it's been really nice catching up, but I have to get back to work."

Fred stood, slipping his hands in the pockets of his khakis as he glanced at the archives she held. "You're doing lots of research on Councilman Randolph. Is he the first subject of your blog?"

"Um, yeah," she said, heart pounding at the mention of Randolph's name. "He's kind of a local celebrity, so I figured, why not?"

Fred's face was impassive as he studied her, and Claire licked her parched lips. Clutching the papers to her breasts, she took a step away until she spotted another man approaching them between the shelves. Dark hair, broad shoulders, and a glare locked directly on her, Claire understood this was the man in black Cyrus had spotted the other day. Fear constricted her throat as she turned to warn Fred.

"Not one step closer," Fred said through gritted teeth, pulling his light summer jacket aside to show the gun on his hip. "We don't want to make a scene, Zander."

"Let her go," the man said, his gaze trailing between Claire and Fred as he pushed aside his sport coat to show a gun upon his belt. "I won't tell you again, Sebastian."

Confused and terrified, Claire stared at Fred. "Sebastian?"

He rolled his eyes. "Come on, Claire. Fred Savage? I can't believe you bought that. I thought you were some sort of super genius scientist or something."

"I don't understand," she said, glancing between the two men. "Who are you?" she asked the stranger.

"That's Zander," Sebastian said, jerking his head toward the man. "He thinks he knows what's going on, but he has no idea." Pulling a syringe from his pocket, he held it up and removed the cap, a menacing look on his face. "I've got two vials of this stuff, and it's nasty, Zander. I'll shoot you so full of it, you'll be incapacitated for a week. Is that what you really want?"

"Claire, I want you to listen to me carefully," Zander said, voice calm as his gaze stayed locked on Sebastian. "Sebastian is aligned with an organization called the Knights of Washington. I've been watching him for some time, as I've been watching you and Cyrus. Your association with Doc Viv doesn't help."

Wheels of confusion fired in Claire's head as she struggled to make sense of the situation. "Doc Viv? What does she have to do with this?"

"Enough," Sebastian said, pulling his gun from its holster. Cocking it, he aimed at Zander, who pulled his own gun. "We've made enough of a scene that people are going to make their way over here. Is that what you want, Zander?"

"My goal is to figure out what you and the Knights are looking to accomplish. And I'm sure as hell not going to let you hurt an innocent woman."

Sebastian's lips formed a cruel smile. "It must drive you crazy that you can't discern my motives. Believe me, you never will."

"Holster your gun and get the hell out of here. I won't ask again," Zander said, standing firm, gun aimed between Sebastian's eyes.

"Careful," Sebastian said, craning his neck. "I think the librarian is coming. Oh, yes, here she is now."

A woman appeared, gasping as she took in the scene of two men aiming guns at each other. "Oh, my, what is going on here?"

"Ma'am," Zander said, holding up a palm to her. "Please stay back."

Sebastian seized the moment, rushing toward Zander and plunging the vial into his neck. The man gasped, clutching his neck as his body fell to the floor.

"Sit in the chair," Sebastian said to the librarian, gesturing with his gun, "or you're next."

The woman rushed to the nearby chair, collapsing into it as she sobbed. Claire stood helpless, wanting to help Zander as he lay limp on the ground, but unable to move since Sebastian had aimed the gun at her.

"I'm keeping my hand on the trigger as we exit the library, Claire," he said, his sneer vile. "If you scream or make one move I don't like, I'll shoot you. Do you understand?"

Frozen with fear, she could barely nod her head.

Sebastian grabbed her forearm, tugging her close, as the forgotten newspapers fell to the floor. With a firm grip, he led her down the stairs. To onlookers, they may as well have been a couple strolling arm in arm. Once they were outside, under the bright morning sun, he walked her to a side street where a white van was parked. Approaching the van, the door slid open.

"What the hell, Sebastian?" a man asked from inside, extending his hand. "You almost got caught."

Claire realized they must've been wearing comm devices in their ears since the man seemed apprised of the situation.

Sebastian pushed her toward him, and he violently grabbed her and tried to drag her inside. Adrenaline kicked in, and she began to struggle. Gun or not, she wasn't letting these assholes take her without a fight.

"Zander was there, do-gooder son of a bitch. Hey!" Sebastian yelled at Claire, grabbing her by the neck and squeezing so hard she fought to breathe. "That's enough out of you." As she twisted her body, trying to escape, she saw him pull another vial from his pocket. Uncapping it, he plunged it into her neck.

"Claire!" Cyrus's voice boomed from far away...so far away...and she attempted to turn her now limp head.

"Cyrus!" she called, barely seeing his large frame in the distance as he ambled toward her on the crutches.

Her body was pulled into the van, and the door slammed tight as tires screeched. And then, all she saw was darkness.

Chapter 15

Cyrus watched the van speed away and unleashed every curse word he'd ever learned. Bending down to pick up the crutch that had fallen to the ground, he strived to keep calm, although fear laced every cell in his frame. There was only one objective in his world now: finding Claire. Heading back toward the main entrance of the library, he decided he'd start by retracing her steps.

As he was about to ascend the steps to the front door, an ambulance pulled up in front of the large building, siren blaring. Not wanting to be discovered, Cyrus ducked behind the corner.

Paramedics pulled a backboard and jump bag from the vehicle and ran inside. Next, a police car arrived, parking behind the ambulance. Cyrus observed two uniformed cops walk up the stairs and into the library. A few minutes later, the paramedics exited, carrying what looked to be an unconscious man. They pulled a stretcher from the ambulance, placed him on it, and lifted the man inside. Curious, Cyrus moved closer.

"Everything okay in the library?" he asked one of the cops who'd followed the paramedics out.

"Everything's fine, sir," he said with a nod. "Please step away from the scene." The cop gestured toward the unconscious man being loaded into the ambulance.

Cyrus almost felt his eyes pop from his head when he recognized the man dressed in black he'd seen the other day. As the wheels in his mind churned, he understood this was no coincidence. The man must have something to do with Claire's kidnapping.

"They'll take him to the closest hospital?" Cyrus asked the cop.

"Yes, sir. To MedStar Washington Hospital. I appreciate your concern, but we're trying to keep the sidewalk clear until the ambulance departs."

"No problem," Cyrus said, armed with the information he needed. He traversed two blocks and hailed a cab, directing the driver to take him to MedStar Hospital. He would make sure he knew exactly which room the man in black was assigned to. And then, they were going to have a little chat.

* * * *

Cyrus stood with his arms crossed, back against the wall, as the man's eyelids fluttered. Uttering a small moan, his lids lifted, and he gazed around the hospital room, appearing disoriented.

"Am I in a hospital?"

"Yes," Cyrus said, arms dropping to his sides as he inched closer on the crutches. "I want you to listen very carefully to me. I have a knife and can gut you in a second. If you scream, you're dead."

The man arched an eyebrow. "That's not necessary, Cyrus. We're on the same side here."

It took every ounce of will for Cyrus to maintain his composure. Shock reverberated through every pore of his frame.

"I want answers. Now." The words were forced through clenched teeth.

The man inhaled, nodding as he assessed the tube in his arm and the hospital band on his wrist. "I tried to prevent her capture. Sebastian works for some really bad people. We need to find her quickly."

"Listen, buddy," Cyrus said, reaching down to squeeze the man's shoulder. *Hard.* "I don't know who the hell you are, but I want to know every ounce of information down to what you had for breakfast. Got it?"

"The vise grip isn't helping," the man said, scowling.

Cyrus released his grip, giving the man a glare. "Talk. Now."

"Man, you're intimidating. Okay, let me break it down to the pertinent parts."

Cyrus gave a curt nod.

"My name is Zander Katz. I was a cop for a few years before I became a private investigator. A few months ago, a man hired me to do some digging on a woman named Dr. Vivian Elders."

Cyrus scowled, trying to figure out what Doc Viv had to do with Claire's kidnapping.

"Dr. Elders has a child, Marie. They wanted me to collect her DNA from discarded cups, swabs—all those things you find in the garbage—but the man had a pretty unsettling vibe. So I began investigating him instead. He ended up being Sebastian Hawthorne, a high-ranking member of a pretty nefarious organization called the Knights of Washington."

"Claire and I uncovered some dirt on them," Cyrus said.

"Well, they're really bad dudes," Zander said, running his hand over his face. "They're a group of extremely well-connected and wealthy men who are intent on oppressing anyone who doesn't believe in their principles. They feel resources and power should only reside with those they've chosen."

"And they got their claws in Councilman Randolph."

Zander tilted his head. "I honestly don't think Randolph is a terrible guy at his core. But he wants their money and will do anything for his donors. He likes being a public official and believes it brings him status he would never achieve as an ordinary member of society. I once heard him tell his wife that once he achieves true power, he'll be able to make his own way and break away from the Knights. Unfortunately, we know plans like this usually never come to fruition."

"Once you take their money, they've got you for life."

"Pretty much."

Cyrus contemplated, arms crossed over his chest. "Why would they kidnap Claire?"

"I don't know," Zander said. "I heard Sebastian discussing it when I was surveilling him. Supposedly, she's going to save Dr. Elder's daughter's life, and they don't want her to succeed. I have no idea how they claim to know of future actions that haven't even happened yet, but they are adamant in this assertion."

Cyrus studied the man, contemplating how much he should divulge about time travel. He deemed Zander honest and believed him, but he might alienate the man if he started talking about the Sphere and the dystopian future. Instead, he needed an ally, and in this world where he knew no one, Zander was his best option.

"Thank you for trying to protect Claire. Obviously, my entire focus will be on finding her. If you're open to helping me, I would welcome it."

"I'm open," Zander said. "I want to shut down these bastards. There's a warehouse where they meet sometimes. It's owned by one of the ranking members of the Knights. I say we start there."

Cyrus cocked his head. "I'll wait for you outside the hospital. The police will want to question you. I waited until the cop guarding your door went to get coffee. I overheard him on the phone with his captain confirming the librarian doesn't want to press charges."

"That's good. I used to be a cop, so I know most of the guys on the force. I'll answer their questions and meet you outside. There's no reason for them to hold me. My gun is registered."

Cyrus nodded and trailed to the lobby, ensuring he blended in and wouldn't be noticed. Once outside, he sat on the bench by the front door, spine straight as he counted every second that ticked by.

"I'm coming, Claire," he said softly, terrified for her safety. "Don't give up."

The hour he spent waiting for Zander to appear was the longest one of his life.

* * * *

Cyrus rubbed his hand over the back of his neck as he sat beside Zander in his beat-up hatchback. They'd taken a taxi back to the library where his car was parked so they could begin the search for Claire. The industrial park was on the outskirts of D.C., and every second seemed to tick by as they meandered along, Zander smoking a cigarette every few minutes as he drove.

"How long have you smoked?" Cyrus asked.

"Too damn long," Zander said, tossing the butt out the window. "Keep telling myself I'll quit but just never seem to find the will to do it."

When they neared their destination, they parked a few blocks from the building where Sebastian was possibly holding Claire hostage. Careful to remain inconspicuous, they weaved through the buildings until they arrived at the back door of the warehouse.

"You wedge the door open, and I'll charge in since I have a firearm," Zander instructed.

"Ten-four."

"You're going to be okay on the ankle?"

Cyrus leaned the crutches against the building. "I can put some weight on it, and, honestly, I'd break it a hundred times to save her. Adrenaline will keep me going. I'll assess it afterward. Her safety is most important."

Giving a nod, Zander lifted his gun, ready to aim. Cyrus turned the knob, realizing it was locked as he'd expected. Concentrating with all his might, he slammed his shoulder into the door, the full force of his two-hundred-and-thirty-pound frame behind it. It banged open, and Zander rushed inside.

Cyrus entered behind him and stared at the dim, empty room. "Where is she?"

"I don't know," Zander said, inching forward. "Doesn't look like anyone's been here in a while. Damn it."

Cyrus wanted to retch at the thought of Claire abducted and in danger. Rage swamped his every muscle as he fought the urge to scream.

"I know," Zander said, patting him on the shoulder. "Not the time to lose it, man. Let's go outside and brainstorm. Come on."

Vowing to remain calm, Cyrus hobbled outside and reclaimed the crutches. Behind the warehouse, they discussed where else Sebastian could've taken Claire.

"There's a meeting hall where they congregate sometimes," Zander said, squinting his eyes. "I've surveilled some of the meetings, which look more like a fascist rally than anything else. Although they don't own the hall, we could try to find her there. If we come up dry, maybe they will have left a clue behind?"

"Let's go."

Twenty minutes later, they arrived at the banquet hall. Since it was early afternoon on a weekday, Cyrus doubted anyone would be inside. They tried the front door, which was locked.

"There's a back door," Zander said, gesturing with his head. "Come on."

They walked down the narrow alley that separated the buildings before coming to a ramp. After trying the knob, which was locked, Cyrus shoved his shoulder into it several times, effectively busting it open.

"While I appreciate your ability to bust down doors, I could've picked the lock," Zander mumbled.

Cyrus scowled as he entered, searching the darkened premises. Zander drew his gun from its holster, and they slowly cased the hall.

"Empty," Zander said, lowering the gun. "Let's look around."

They found discarded pamphlets in the kitchen, and Cyrus lifted one, anger welling in his chest.

"**Knights of Washington: The Best of Society**," he read from the pamphlet. Scoffing, he crumpled it and threw it on the counter. "Not even close."

They searched the musty basement below the building, not finding anything, and Cyrus worked to suppress his fear. Understanding he had to remain calm, he asked, "Do you have an office you work out of with internet access?"

"Yes," Zander said, waving him toward the stairs that led above. "It's slow as hell, but it should get the job done. Come on."

Before they could move, Cyrus heard a gun cock from behind. Pivoting, every muscle was alert as he scanned the room, unable to see in the dimness.

"Who's there?" he called, slowly inching forward. Sensing Zander behind him, he advanced toward the corner from which the sound had originated.

Suddenly, a body flashed before him, the man running for dear life. Cyrus grabbed the man's wrist, jerking him close and landing a solid punch on the guy's cheek. He emitted a grunt and attempted to lift his gun, which Cyrus effectively knocked from his hand. The man stumbled over the fallen crutches, now flanking them, and Cyrus seized his other wrist. Pushing the guy to his knees, Cyrus held his arms in a death grip behind his back.

"Where is she?" he gritted in the man's ear.

"Fuck you!"

Cyrus twisted the man's arm to the point where it was ready to snap. "Don't make me break it. Tell me where she is."

When he remained silent, Zander came into view, gun lifted. "This is Michael Lowe, an associate of Sebastian's."

Recognition washed over Cyrus. "You were the man who dragged Claire inside the van. Tell me where she is. Now!"

"Sebastian sent me to keep an eye on you. I'm more scared of the Knights than I am of you," Michael said, panting as he struggled. "You can kill me, but I'm not telling you anything."

Frustrated, Cyrus grabbed his wrists in one hand and clutched Michael's thick hair. "I won't ask you again."

"Sebastian has her, and her fate is sealed. I'm not talking."

Filled with rage, Cyrus dropped to his knees and pushed him to the floor, smashing his face into the dirty concrete. Dragging Michael's head from the ground, he realized he'd knocked the man unconscious.

"Well, he's certainly not talking now," Zander said.

"Damn it," Cyrus uttered, leaving the man crumpled on the floor as he grabbed the crutches and stood.

"You're a hell of a fighter, man."

"Where I come from, you have to be." Running his hand over his head, slick with sweat, Cyrus felt utterly defeated. "Let's leave him here. He should regain consciousness soon, but he'll have a hell of a headache. Or maybe one of the members of the Knights will find him and know we mean business. In the meantime, let's do the internet search. Hopefully, we can find something."

Zander reached down and grabbed Michael's gun. "I'll take prints from this and have my contacts at the station run them. Maybe I'll get lucky and the serial number won't be scratched off, but I doubt it. Come on."

Determined, Cyrus followed his new ally.

Chapter 16

Claire recovered consciousness, although she felt incredibly groggy. Rubbing her forehead, she recalled the events from earlier, thankful she could remember them. Fred was really Sebastian, a grade A douche who'd kidnapped and drugged her. Squishing her features together, she imagined throwing a steaming caramel macchiato right into his face. Oh yes, she'd figure out a way to do that one day if it killed her.

Sitting up, she realized she was in a hotel room. Two double beds, one of which she sat upon, took up most of the space in the small room. Looking around, she saw the phone atop the bedside table, complete with a freshly cut cord. Well, looked like she wasn't phoning home anytime soon.

Standing, she balanced by holding the nightstand, still a bit woozy. Closing her eyes, she remembered Cyrus running toward her, a look of such distress on his face as he'd called to her.

"Thank god you saw me, chief," she muttered. "Hope you find me soon." She was certain of one thing: Cyrus wouldn't rest until he found her. Thankful for that knowledge, she figured she could also try to find a way out of her predicament.

She searched the room, finding nothing but an old Bible and some pamphlets about sights to see in Washington D.C. The bathroom didn't fare much better until she began searching the shelves under the sink and found a shiny pair of toenail clippers that someone must've left behind. Sliding open the file, she noticed the pointed edge.

"Bingo."

Armed with her newfound weapon, she continued to search the room, coming up empty. Tentatively approaching the door, she flipped the bolt and slowly turned the knob, her heartbeat quickening as it creaked open. Was it really going to be this easy? So close to escape, she yanked open the door.

"Hello, Claire," Sebastian said, stepping into her path and arching a brow. "I see you're awake." Lifting his gun, he gestured her back inside. "Let's go."

Shooting him a hate-filled glare, she returned to sit on the bed. "Why did you kidnap me? What the hell is going on?"

Steeping inside the room, he closed the door and bolted it, causing bile to rise in her throat. If he even tried to touch her, she'd scream and fight like hell.

"Don't worry," he said, giving her a dismissive look. "I'm not going to attack you. Fat girls really aren't my type."

She wanted to tell him to fuck off but kept her lips sealed. Lewis had run several drills simulating soldier attacks at the hub when he was alive, and the main lesson had always been to retain your wits and look for an opening. Captors reveled in the power dynamic they created and thrived off their victims' fear. Straightening her shoulders, she kept her expression void of emotion.

"You don't seem to want to kill me, or I'd probably already be dead."

"Very good," he said, nodding. "It's important you stay alive because your daughter will become a very important member of President Randolph's staff one day. Her efforts are integral to ensuring he wins the election."

Realization washed over her, heavy and thick, as she comprehended this man was also a time traveler. How many others were there? How had they gotten access to the time machine? And even more mind-blowing: she would eventually have a daughter who would align with Randolph? No fucking way. Not if Claire had anything to say about it.

"I see the questions firing in your mind. You won't get any answers from me. I'm here to stop you from saving Vivian Elders' bastard daughter, and then you can go on with your pointless life."

Claire closed her eyes, the ringing in her ears so loud she had to restrain from screaming. Sliding her hand in her pocket, she squeezed the clippers.

"I know about the clippers, Claire. You find them in every timeline, and then you attempt to stab them in my neck. I wouldn't do it, by the way. I end up pistol whipping you, and you get a pretty terrible shiner. I admire your spunk, but let's not—"

Claire leaped from the bed and shoved the pointed file of the clippers directly into his crotch. Sebastian's eyes grew wide before he dropped the gun and clutched his groin, falling to the ground. Picking up the gun, she aimed it at him as he writhed on the floor.

"You know what Lewis always taught us?" she asked, holding the gun with outstretched arms, barrel pointed at his face, both arms quaking.

"That if we realized we were in a loop, to let go of our fears and react completely opposite of how we wanted to. Yes, my first thought was to plunge it into your neck, but I like this twist much better. Good luck fucking anyone now, fat or not, asshole!" Kicking him once more in the stomach, she unlatched the door and bolted from the room.

Judging by the sun, it was late afternoon. Claire peered over the balcony railing and searched for the van below, wondering if Sebastian's associate was near. When she didn't spot it, she sprang into action. Adrenaline coursed through her, along with compulsion to flee the area. She couldn't ask for help at the front desk since they'd most likely call the police and she wanted to avoid that at all costs. Noting the room number, she trailed down the concrete stairs and ran along the busy road next to the hotel.

Eventually, she was able to flag down a taxi and made sure the gun was stuffed in her waistband, so she didn't freak the guy out.

"Where to, ma'am?" the driver asked.

She gave him the address of the Taco Bell five blocks from home, just in case creepy van dude was following her. She'd debilitated Sebastian pretty damn well, but that would probably make him more intent on finding her. When the driver pulled into the parking lot, she climbed out and searched every surrounding angle. Not seeing the van, she jumped back in.

"Actually, my cash is at home. Duh. Can you take me there?" Giving him the address, she clenched the door handle, terrified but needing to get to home base to reset.

After running up the stairs, grabbing a twenty, and handing it to the driver, she headed inside and locked everything behind her. Cyrus wasn't home, and she figured he was probably out looking for her. Sebastian now had her phone, which they shared, so he didn't even have one to call. Walking to the sink, she washed her face with shaking hands, realizing how close she'd come to being in serious danger. Once she'd had a few minutes to calm down, she sat down in the chair beside the couch, booted up the laptop, and got to work.

* * * *

Cyrus felt utterly defeated as he ambled up the stairs on the crutches he was coming to detest. Hopelessness consumed him as he stuck his key in the deadbolt lock, turning it before doing the same with the knob. Pushing open the door, he took in the sight before him and almost fainted in relief.

Claire sat on the floor surrounded by a multitude of yellow papers, all with her succinct scribble, torn haphazardly from the notepad she held in her lap. Peering over her shoulder, she beamed.

"Hey, chief." She gave a wave. "About time. I was getting worried."

Expelling a huge sigh of relief, he closed the door and maneuvered toward her, throwing the crutches aside and lowering to his knees. Cupping her face in his hands, his eyes darted between hers.

"How did you escape?"

"Did you doubt me? You know me better than to think I'd let some second-rate criminals keep me hostage for long."

"Oh, my god," he breathed, staring at the ceiling as he struggled to regulate his heartbeat. "I was so worried."

"I know," she said, encircling his wrist as he held her face. "I knew you wouldn't rest until you found me. But I also figured I should try to escape. Surprise! I'm pretty badass."

A laugh escaped his throat. "You're so fucking badass, Finch. What happened?"

She told him everything down to the last detail, particularly adamant when she explained how she'd gotten the upper hand on Sebastian. "He told me I stabbed him in the neck in every timeline, so I tried to change it up. I stuck the file right through his dick, Cyrus, and I'm pretty sure I caught some ball too. Fucking bastard. He's never going to pee straight again."

Cyrus embraced her, overcome with joy that she was alive and unharmed. "Damn, woman. Don't ever come near me with a pair of toenail clippers." Drawing back, he couldn't contain his grin. "And I mean, *ever*."

"Ten-four," she said, giving him a teasing salute. "He deserved it. Kidnapped me *and* called me fat. Screw him. He was definitely no Brad Pitt either."

Cyrus's eyebrows drew together.

"Saw his picture in one of Doc Viv's waiting room magazines," she said, waving a dismissive hand. "Hot. Like, Hunter Rhodes hot."

"Rhodes isn't that hot. He's short, and I'm pretty sure his teeth will fall out one day from chewing those damn toothpicks."

"Everyone is short compared to you, Cyrus. You're six-six, for god's sake. I think he's six-two. And he's hot, believe me. You're not jealous, are you?"

"No," he lied.

"Holy crap! You're jealous of Captain McHotty Pants! Don't worry, you're way hotter than he is. I promise." She drew an X over her heart.

The words elated him, although they shouldn't have since he'd vowed to never touch her again. He studied her, realizing they now had a plethora of problems that didn't exist before. It was worrisome, and he struggled with how to move forward.

"I know," she said, shaking her head as she looked at the pages strewn around her. "I'm doing my best to compile all the information I have. I can probably track down Sebastian's last name through searches or even possibly through hacking into the hotel database. I took note of the room number, and it was either in his name, his associate's, or a fake name. Either way, it's worth checking out. I was never as competent with hacking as Zach, and the internet is shit in 2002, but I have some tricks up my sleeve. It won't be easy, but I want to try to put together a framework of everything we know about him, especially since he traveled here like we did."

"Hawthorne. Sebastian's last name is Hawthorne." Cyrus brought her up to speed on his interactions with Zander. "He seems like a good guy, and I trust him as much as I trust anyone right now. Also, being a P.I., he has a lot of resources at his fingertips."

"Ohhh, do you think he wants to join **Montgomery and Finch, π's for Hire**?" she teased.

Cyrus playfully rolled his eyes. "I think he's all set in his own firm. I'm in though. Let's take down these bastards. First, we need to get a new cell phone."

"Definitely. Should we find a new place to stay? What if they try to attack us here?"

Cyrus contemplated, understanding finding a new place without documentation where they could pay cash would be difficult. "This area is highly trafficked by police, and if we move somewhere else, they'll probably track us there. I say we stay and remain on high alert. I'm also going to ask Zander to secure a gun for me."

Reaching under the couch, she slid the gun over and extended it to him. "Like this one?"

"You stole his gun? Right on." Taking it, he inspected the magazine and made sure the safety was on.

"Told you, I decimated the bastard."

Awed by her, he shook his head and set the gun on the table. Her teeth fidgeted with her bottom lip as questions loomed in her eyes.

"What is it?"

"So we're going to stay together, right? I don't want to live apart from you, especially now."

Cyrus nodded. "We're staying together now that we're under serious threat. I promise I'll be a perfect gentleman."

"I'd expect nothing less from you," she said softly, her expression wistful.

"Claire," he whispered, unable to resist the urge to touch her. Running his hand over her hair, he stared deep into her eyes. "I don't want to hurt you. That's why we can't act on our attraction. I wish you could understand. We're just too different, sweetheart, and want different things."

Her tongue darted across her lips, causing arousal to flare in his gut. "I'm open to discussing how we can overcome those differences, Cyrus."

He remained silent, cursing his undeniable desire for her. It was terrifying because it was one of the few things in his well-ordered existence he was unable to control.

"Holy shit," she whispered, shaking her head. "I've never seen you so scared. It's...well, it's pretty awesome. It means you really care."

"I'm not scared," he muttered, "and of course I care."

Her lips curved into a grin. "I'm going to have to get laid again one day. Might as well be with you."

The thought of anyone else touching her smooth skin make him want to punch his fist through the wall. Frowning at the possessiveness, he sighed.

"We have to remain platonic, Claire. Especially now that these bastards are on our tails. I want this situation resolved."

She squinted one eye, sizing him up. "Me too. And if you know anything about me, you'll know that I'm definitely not letting this go." Standing, she offered her hand. "Come on. Let's go get a new phone and contact Zander. We've got a lot of stuff to accomplish."

Taking her hand, he hobbled to his feet and located the crutches, wondering how in the hell she'd somehow gotten the upper hand. Wily woman. As he followed her from the apartment, taken by the swells of her gorgeous ass, he wondered how long he could fight their indisputable attraction. Judging by the fact every ounce of blood was surging to his shaft, he realized he was already doomed.

Chapter 17

Claire and Cyrus sat in Zander's office as the man furiously punched the keyboard with two extended fingers. Tongue situated between his teeth, he glared at the screen.

"I can take the reins if you need," Claire said, taking pity on him. "I'm a pretty good typer. My friend Zach taught me years ago."

"I'm good," he said, his mask of frustration contradicting his words. "One day, we're going to have technology that doesn't make us wait forever. Buffering. Always buffering."

Claire and Cyrus shared a look, acknowledging his words were truer than he could even know.

"Okay," he said, sitting back and running a hand through his hair. "I pulled up all the pictures I've taken. I emailed them to a dedicated AOL account just in case anything happened to me. The login and password are in an envelope in this drawer," he said, tapping the side of his desk, "so the police would find it if they searched. Come on over and have a look."

He stood from his chair and gestured for Claire to sit when she stepped around. Cyrus and Zander stood over her shoulder as she clicked through the pictures.

"Most of these are images of Doc Viv speaking with Randolph," Claire said. "I don't understand their connection. They seem to have very different ideals since she treats the underserved, and he's involved in an organization that's trying to eradicate them."

"Exactly," Zander said. Leaning on the desk, he crossed his arms over his chest. "Several years ago, there was a rumor Edward had an affair with someone during his engagement to Alice Cramwell. The woman's identity was never revealed. I think it was Vivian Elders."

"Whoa," Claire breathed, her eyes growing wide. "Doc Viv and Randolph? Heavy."

Zander nodded. "I think her daughter might be Edward's. It would make sense why his donors hired me to collect DNA on Marie."

"Having an illegitimate daughter while he was engaged to his current wife—and one who spends her life fighting for those his donors detest—could severely impact his chances of political advancement," Cyrus said.

"Bingo." Zander stood and paced as he continued. "People who invest their money in political candidates want a return on their investment. These photos show Vivian and Edward involved in heated discussions. Perhaps he's trying to help her. Maybe he's threatening her. It's possible he still cares for her and wants to protect her and Marie."

"Does he help her financially?" Claire asked.

"Not from any paper trail I can find, but that doesn't mean anything. Vivian was involved with another man named Jonathan Reeves directly after her relationship with Edward. It's possible Edward thinks Marie is that man's child. I have no proof she's Edward's, but even the possibility of him having these loose ends would be worrisome to his donors. In my experience, powerful men will stop at nothing to advance candidates they think will do their bidding."

"Sebastian mentioned holding me captive so I couldn't save Marie. Sounds like something big is supposed to go down and I'm going to prevent it. Man, I just keep getting more badass. I think I like 2002 Me. Heck yes!" Holding her hand high, she smacked it with her other one, giving herself a high-five.

"It's great you're badass and all," Zander said, "but how in the hell could they possibly know you were going to save Marie? I've worked with psychics in my past, but none of them were *that* good."

Claire and Cyrus spared each other a glance before she stood. Gesturing to the chair, she said, "Have a seat, Zander. We're about to blow this case wide open."

"I'm fine."

"Believe me," Cyrus said, ambling over to cup the man's shoulder and gently push him to the chair. "You're going to want to sit down for this."

Expelling a breath, he sat and looked up at them expectantly. "Okay, go for it."

Claire glanced at Cyrus, and he nodded, indicating she should proceed.

"Zander, first of all, thank you for helping me. For helping us. It's really awesome because we don't know a lot of people in this timeline."

"Timeline," he repeated, eyebrows drawn together. "I was happy to help. These are some bad dudes."

"They sure are. In fact, they're most likely the precursor to a very evil regime that will gain power once President Randolph destroys the world."

"President Randolph destroys the world," he murmured.

"Yes," she said. "It's probably best if you just listen and don't repeat everything I say." When he nodded, she continued. "Let me start by telling you about September 4, 2035. You see, that was the day history changed forever..."

Thirty minutes later, Zander stared up at them, wide-eyed, as he digested everything they'd just unloaded on him. Leaning down, Claire placed a supportive hand on his upper arm.

"You doing okay there, buddy?" Searching for his reaction, she noticed his vein pulsing in his neck.

"Okay, I think I've got it," he said, leaning back in the chair and running a hand through his thick black hair. "You two are members of a post-apocalyptic scientific team from 2075 who invented a time machine to travel to 2035 and prevent future President Randolph from detonating the nukes. But the time machine malfunctioned, and you were sent to 2002 instead. You looked up Vivian Elders because Marie is an eighty-year-old member of your team in 2075. You're stuck here until Randolph's granddaughter comes to save you, if she ever does."

Claire looked at Cyrus, and they both shrugged. Turning back to him, they said in unison, "Yes."

Zander expelled a heavy breath through his lips. "Wow. I need a minute. Half of me thinks you're certifiably insane, and half of me thinks it makes perfect damn sense. Holy shit."

"It explains why Sebastian knows the future. I have no idea how he ended up here or who sent him back, but it was probably Victor Hernandez."

"The bad guy who expands the evil regime. Right. Well, why don't we just find him in 2002 and steer him on another path?"

"So, a few things," Claire said, leaning her hip on the desk. "First of all, Victor isn't even alive yet. Judging by the scant information Lainey told me after Eli revealed himself as a spy, Victor was in his late twenties in 2035. That means he'll be born sometime in the latter half of this decade."

"Okay, so we'll find his mother."

"It doesn't work that way. I know this is hard to comprehend, but the space-time continuum is really intricate and fragile. You can't just go back and kill someone in the past to stop future events. That just creates a paradox that ultimately destroys everything and usually ends up abolishing that timeline. Instead, you have to go back and change small things along the way so you don't end up creating a butterfly effect that drastically upends the world."

"But you were planning to stop Randolph in 2035?"

"Yes," Claire said. "The consequences of his actions are so disastrous that taking the calculated risk of stopping him is warranted. But it's important he be allowed to ascend to power and get to the point where he's in the bunker so the team can confront him. If we just shot him now, it would set off a ton of other small discrepancies in this timeline that would very quickly change the entire fabric of space-time. The world most likely wouldn't survive. I know this doesn't make a hell of a lot of sense, but, trust me, there's a systematic plan that needs to be followed. Lewis went over it with us in detail for many years."

Zander remained silent, contemplating her words.

"She's pretty much a genius," Cyrus said, lifting a shoulder above his crossed arms. "I'd listen to her. It's never really made a whole lot of sense to me either, but I trust Claire. She's the smartest person I've ever met."

"Thanks," she said, feeling herself blush at his compliment. "Lainey's the real genius, but I try."

"You're both pretty damn amazing," he said, giving her a wink.

As her heart melted, she smiled at Zander. "So now that we've brought you up to date on the craziest story you'll probably ever hear, what are your thoughts? Still want to help us?"

"Yes," Zander said, standing and walking over to a cabinet that sat against the side wall. Pulling out a handgun and several boxes of ammunition, he glanced at Cyrus. "I'm guessing you'll want a gun?"

"Actually," Cyrus said, lifting his shirt to expose his waist, "Claire stole Sebastian's. But I'd love a holster."

Zander's eyebrows lifted. "Well done."

"Thanks," she said, giving a satisfied shrug.

"I've always followed my gut, and it hasn't let me down yet. I feel something pulling me toward this case. I have since those bastards approached me asking me to do surveillance on a little girl. That's just not right. Let's take 'em down."

"I overheard Edward speaking to someone in the alley when we were spying on him. Now that I think about it, I'm pretty sure he was referring to Doc Viv on the call. Something about how she'd ruin everything, and he'd talk to her."

"I have my follow-up appointment tomorrow," Cyrus said. "We'll talk to her and see if we can get her to inadvertently divulge any info. We'll be in touch afterward."

"Sounds good," Zander said.

* * * *

Once they were home, they sat on the couch contemplating the strange turn their new reality had taken.

"Sebastian's going to be pissed," Claire said, trying to tamp down the fear. "I really went for it. If I were him, I'd want to murder me."

"No one's going to touch a hair on your head," Cyrus said, pulling her into his side.

"Except you," she said, snuggling into him.

"Except me. Platonically."

She smiled, sliding her arms around his torso. God, she loved the feel of him against her. "For now." The cadence of his breathing was a calming force against her cheek. "I think I'm coming to realize I might have to seduce you, chief."

"It's not happening, Finch," he said, stroking her hair. Closing her eyes, she reveled in his caresses.

"You're already toast. Just wait. I'll figure you out."

His deep chuckle reverberated through her body. Exhausted from the events of the extremely long day, she fell asleep against his chest within minutes. Later, she awoke to his awkward motions as he placed her in the bed and covered her with the blankets.

"You carried me?" she asked, worriedly glancing at his ankle.

"It's fine," he said, lowering to place a chaste kiss on her forehead. "I can put some weight on it. Sweet dreams."

"I'm too heavy," she mumbled, pulling the comforter under her chin as her lids cemented shut, elated by his whispered words before he left her to the darkness.

"You're perfect, Claire."

For some reason, when spoken from his lips, the words rang true in her heart.

Chapter 18

The next morning, Claire and Cyrus sat in front of Doc Viv's desk as she pointed to his most recent X-ray against the wall.

"Everything is healing really nicely, Cyrus. I see you making a full recovery." Switching off the backlight, she removed the film and sat down behind the desk. "I recommend you go ahead and keep putting weight on it with the aid of the crutches until you feel you don't need them anymore. Maybe another week or two at most. I still want you to wear the air cast for a few weeks, even once you lose the crutches, and after that, you can buy a really firm ankle brace at the drugstore. Carolyn at the front desk will recommend a few brands to you."

"When should I expect to walk normally again?"

"You'll limp for a few more weeks even with the air cast and subsequent ankle brace. After that, hopefully we'll see vast improvement. It will continue to swell, especially at night, and ice is a good remedy for that."

"Thanks, Doc," Cyrus said, seeming relieved. "I'll make sure to get the recommendations from Carolyn, although I missed seeing your daughter at the front desk today."

"Yes, I actually made Marie go to school today, which led to a wonderfully intense argument to start the day. Don't ever have kids. They'll drive you nuts."

Claire and Cyrus chuckled.

"Obviously, I'm kidding," she said, playfully rolling her eyes. "She's the center of my world."

"This might be way too personal, and if it is, please tell me to stuff it, but how does Marie's father feel about her taking days off from school to work at the clinic?" Claire asked.

Vivian licked her lips, her eyes narrowing slightly.

"I'm sorry," Claire said, feeling she might have pushed the kind woman too far. "It's none of my business. You've been so amazing, Doc Viv, and I have a huge mouth. Ask Cyrus. Drives him nuts."

"Only ninety-nine percent of the time," he muttered.

Vivian seemed to relax as she assessed them. "It's fine. I guess it's a natural question. There is no father. I chose to have Marie through artificial insemination. Realized a while ago that I was terrible with men, and you know the old saying about trying the same thing over and over and expecting different results. So I just stopped dating. Honestly, it's allowed me to focus on my work, and that truly fulfills me, along with being a mom."

Claire nodded, pasting on a smile as she wondered why Vivian was lying. She'd bet anything Marie was conceived the old-fashioned way. Making a mental note to work with Zander to research and confirm, she realized it was probably easier to lie. After all, if you told everyone you conceived by artificial insemination, no one would ever question who the father was.

"Well, that's awesome. I'm glad you've found happiness. Marie is such an amazing little girl. I hope we get to see her again soon."

"Well, you're welcome to come to our fundraiser on Friday if you want," she said, handing her a flyer. "It's this fancy thing where physicians get together and raise money for several clinics in the D.C. area. I'm bringing Marie as my plus-one. There will be several local politicians there, news crews, and all that jazz. I know you all don't have a ton of money or fancy clothes, but I get twenty free tickets to give to my patients each year. Surprisingly, I have trouble filling all the spots. I think it's because my patients absolutely hate being around stuffy rich people," she said, wrinkling her nose. "I mean, who doesn't? Anyway, I have several vouchers left, and there will be a ton of free buffet food. Just let Carolyn know if you want to attend, and she'll give you the tickets."

Claire was about to burst with excitement at their good fortune. Glancing at the flyer, she noticed Councilman Randolph was pictured as one of the political attendees. It would be a perfect scenario to observe him with Doc Viv.

"You had me at 'free buffet,'" Claire said, causing the doc to chuckle. "We made a new friend in the area and would love to bring him too, but only if you have enough tickets."

"Like I said, my patients don't really care for these things, so you can certainly have three tickets. The donors don't really like having the patients there either, but I insist on it because they represent who they're funding. Snobby donors usually like to pat themselves on the back for being charitable but don't want to mingle with the very people they help.

It's absolutely ridiculous, but I need their dough, so I'm stuck." Standing, she picked up Cyrus's chart and handed it to him. "If you need anything else, just call the office or ask Carolyn. There's a thrift store on Bryant Street that has fantastic stuff. You should be able to find a nice dress and a suit there if you want. If not, come in jeans and sneakers for all I care. See you there."

"Thank you, Doc," Cyrus said, trailing out of the office on his crutches as Claire followed behind.

Once they were set and armed with three tickets, they strolled outside on high alert in case Sebastian was watching. They'd both discussed the danger they faced and felt the chances of attack were low in broad daylight. After all, nefarious societies often hid in the shadows and wreaked their havoc in secret.

"Great job getting a ticket for Zander too," Cyrus said.

"I'm telling you," she said, shaking the tickets in her hand, "I'm pretty awesome at this whole espionage-P.I.-secret agent thing."

"A super-genius and a super-spy. I'm not sure 2002 is ready for you, Claire."

"Well, 2002 had better get ready," she said, feeling damn proud of herself. "I'm coming for them. All of them."

"All of whom?" he asked, a sparkle in his brown eyes.

"Everyone who tries to fuck with us. I don't know, chief. I think we landed here for a reason. I feel like a superhero or something all of a sudden. Maybe it was crushing that asshole's junk." She shrugged. "But I'm kicking ass and taking names. That's for damn sure."

"Never doubted you for a second, Finch," was his soft, reverent reply as they ambled down the gray sidewalk.

Biting her lip, she gazed up at him. "Are you ready for this badass 'new me?'" She made quotation marks with her fingers. "I'm not sure you can handle it."

His irises raked over her, filled with emotion and desire, and she thought she might pass out right there on the sidewalk. Cyrus had never looked at her with such undisguised passion, but she slowly felt the sexual dynamic in their relationship changing and, damn, but she *loved* it.

"No comment," he muttered, staring ahead as he carried on.

Oh, yeah, he was wound tight as a spring. Feeling like a fucking queen, she basked in her newfound confidence. Claire Finch was no longer the secondary character of her own life. She was the hero and was ready to act like it.

Chapter 19

That Friday evening, Cyrus fiddled with the tie he'd bought at the thrift store. He'd surreptitiously pulled the young male clerk aside and asked him to show him how to tie it since he'd never worn one in his post-apocalyptic existence, but now he barely remembered the lesson. Tugging at the silk in frustration, he decided he didn't need a damn tie anyway.

Claire stepped out of the bedroom, and his heart fell to his knees, which were about three seconds from buckling. She'd pulled her hair into some sort of updo, showcasing her apple-ripe cheekbones. They reddened slightly as she lifted her hands.

"Well?"

The dress was purple, which he knew was one of her favorite colors, and it magnified the green in her eyes so they looked like emeralds set in her heart-shaped face. She didn't have a stitch of makeup on—he couldn't recall her ever wearing any—but someone with Claire's natural beauty didn't need it. The dress flared at her hips and flowed to her knees. Smooth skin led to sparkly shoes she'd purchased along with the dress.

"Okay, it looks terrible. I get it. You don't have to say anything."

"I, uh…"

"It's fine," she said, waving her hand. "It's fun to dress up anyway. Here, let me help you."

As she moved toward him and grabbed the tie, he had the urge to twine each end around her wrists, tie her to the bed, and show her *exactly* how fantastic she looked. With his mouth. On every inch of her skin.

Clearing his throat, he said, "You look nice."

She shot him a droll look as she maneuvered the tie. When it was perfectly knotted, she patted it with her fingers.

"There. You put Captain McHotty Pants to shame."

He breathed a laugh. "How did you learn to do that?"

"Mom and Dad were old-school. Taught me everything before they passed away. How to tie a tie, how to sew, how to gut a fish."

"Wow. Who knew? You could've helped Marie prepare the fish Lewis caught for years."

"Ew," she said, scrunching her nose. "Just because I *know* how to do it doesn't mean I *want* to."

"Fair enough." Throwing on the sport coat, he asked, "You ready?"

Nodding, she picked up the little purse she'd found at the drugstore. Sliding the crutches under his arms and careful to avoid the gun hidden under his waistband, they headed out to call a cab. After picking up Zander at his office, the three of them arrived at the function, noticing the huge sign above the doors that read, "**D.C. Cares 2002.**"

Pulling the tickets from her purse, Claire handed them to the front door staff, and they entered the building. People buzzed around inside dressed in gowns and tuxedos, and Cyrus tugged at his sport coat, feeling like an interloper.

"Wow, these people are super-fancy," Claire said, scanning the crowd.

"And super-white," Cyrus said.

"Yeah. Bummer for such a multicultural city like D.C."

"My granddad told me stories from before the apocalypse. Racism was rampant, systemic, and often unrecognized by the white people it benefited. After Randolph blew up the world, it was passed on and amplified in different ways."

Claire stared up at him, questions swirling in her eyes. "I heard what an ass Captain Parker was when he confronted you in the kitchen at the hub. You'd think after the world was destroyed, everyone could just see each other as human."

"You're giving humanity a lot of credit," he said, scanning the room.

"I see Vivian," Zander said, craning his neck to look across the room. "And Councilman Randolph is sitting over there beside Alice. Guess they left baby Lewis at home."

"Okay, the number one goal is to see if we can catch Randolph and Doc Viv in a private conversation. We need to know if Randolph has any idea Marie might be his daughter, or if he knows the Knights are trying to dig up that information."

"Once we figure out what Randolph knows, we'll forge ahead and hopefully ensure Vivian and Marie's safety," Zander said.

Claire held a finger in the air. "Thus fulfilling my time-traveling superhero prophecy."

"I like it," Zander said, flashing her a grin. "Let's mingle."

*** * * ***

They found the bar, where Claire ordered a glass of wine while Cyrus and Zander ordered bottles of beer. Feeling something tugging at her dress, she glanced down to find Marie.

"So did you come here to spy on me again?"

Claire arched a brow. "Maybe. Have you done anything spy-worthy?"

Marie pursed her lips. "Maybe."

"Oh, yeah?"

She shrugged. "Like, maybe I didn't lose my report card but told Mom I did so she wouldn't see I got a B minus."

"A B minus isn't so bad."

"Tell that to her," she said, jerking her head over to where Vivian stood a few feet away speaking to some donors. "I think she wants me to be a doctor too. I don't really want to though."

"What would you rather do?" Claire asked, thoroughly enjoying their conversation.

"Well," she said, squinting one eye, "I'm really good at normal things. Like, I cook dinner for us most of the time because Mom's always too tired to do it. And I do laundry and clean the house because she gives me an extra five dollars' allowance every time I do it. I know that probably sounds weird, but I like it when things are, uh..." She trailed off, trying to find the word.

"Orderly?"

"Yeah," she said, shrugging. "I guess."

"There's a beauty in order," Claire said, repeating words Older Marie had spoken to her many times. The woman had certainly run a tight ship on the hub and was solely responsible for ensuring the place ran smoothly. Effectively, she'd been the CEO of the compound, coordinating meals and many other daily functions so Lainey and the team could achieve success. "I think you'll find your place one day and figure out how to harness your gifts. And your mom was just telling us the other day how much she loves you. I know she'd be happy with any profession you choose."

"Yeah," she said, kicking the floor with the toe of her cute shoe. "Don't tell her about the report card."

"My lips are sealed." Claire slid her fingers over her lips, mimicking zipping them shut.

"I'm so glad Marie found you," Vivian said, breezing over, glass in hand. "Claire and Cyrus were asking about you the other day, Marie."

"Because Claire's a spy," Marie blurted out, causing Claire to almost choke on her drink.

"Of course, she is," Vivian said, sparing Claire a playful glance. "And what about Cyrus?"

"He's fine, I guess. Haven't sized him up yet."

Chuckling, Cyrus bent down and rested his hands on his knees. "I'm watching out for you, Marie. You're lethal."

Marie beamed at him before turning to Vivian. "Can I have another soda?"

"One more," she said with a nod. "Go on and order it from the bar."

"I'm too short. The bartender didn't see me for ten minutes last time."

"I'll go with you," Cyrus said, extending his hand. "He'll definitely see me."

Marie clutched his hand, and they strode off, Cyrus leaving one crutch behind as he held the girl's hand. Claire was immediately swamped with visions of him holding their own child's hand, smiling down at her with love. God, the image was so real...and something she desperately craved. She'd always wanted children of her own, but to have Cyrus's children? She'd give up every other dream she'd ever imagined to share that with him.

Sebastian's words flitted through her mind. *"It's important you stay alive because your daughter will become a very important member of President Randolph's staff one day. Her efforts are integral to ensuring he wins the election."* Apparently, in whatever timeline Sebastian came from, she had a daughter. The thought was overwhelming, causing her heart to pulse in her chest. Was it possible Cyrus was the father? Wheels churned in her mind as she attempted to postulate a scenario wherein that was even possible, coming up with zilch.

"Hello," Vivian said to Zander.

"Oh, good lord," Claire said, slapping her forehead. "I'm so sorry. Dr. Vivian Elders, this is Zander Katz. He's the friend I was telling you about."

"Hi, Dr. Elders," he said, shaking her hand. "I've heard great things from Cyrus and Claire."

"Well, Cyrus is a model patient. If they could all be that easy." The shake lingered as they smiled into each other's eyes, and realization dawned on Claire. There was an unseen energy emanating between them that was undeniable. *Interesting.*

"Well, I need to top off my wine. Be back in a minute."

Rushing over to Marie and Cyrus, she slapped his arm.

"Ow," he said, scowling at her.

"Holy, er, crap!" she whispered, remembering Marie could hear.

"I know the word 'shit,'" she said matter-of-factly as she stuck a straw in her soda.

"Don't say that word until you're older, young lady," Claire scolded. Looking back at Cyrus, she said, "Doc Viv and Zander are into each other! Look!"

He glanced over and lifted his brows. "Hey. Nice."

"He's easy on the eyes," Marie said, sipping from the straw, "that's for sure. Good job, Mom."

Claire couldn't stop her laugh. "And what do you know about that?"

"Adam Goldstein kissed me under the monkey bars last month. It's no big deal."

"Oh, my god," Claire said, covering her mouth with her hand. "This conversation is so much right now. I can't."

"Whatever." Marie rolled her eyes. "I'm going to go sit with Carolyn. See you guys later. Thanks for helping me with the bartender, Cyrus."

She stomped off as Claire attempted to regain her composure. As she lifted her hands in amused exasperation, he shook his head.

"Unbelievable. I guess you can take the girl out of the dystopian future, but Marie will always be Marie."

Claire bit her lip. "Guess so."

Eventually, they were herded to their tables for dinner. Claire had two helpings of the buffet, deciding she was walking a lot now and that was just damn fine. She also made a plate for Cyrus so he wouldn't have to hobble on one foot. Vivian, Marie, and Carolyn sat at the table in front of them, and a man took the podium to address the crowd.

"Thank you all so much for attending this year's fundraiser. I'm extremely honored to introduce our keynote speaker. This young man has a bright future in politics, and I expect him to remember me when he becomes president one day." Chuckles sprinkled through the crowd as Claire shot Cyrus a knowing look. "Ladies and gentlemen, please welcome Councilman Edward James Randolph."

The room erupted in applause as Edward took the podium. He appeared confident and smooth—every bit the politician—as he spoke about supporting the underserved in D.C.

"Do you think he believes anything he's actually saying?" she whispered to Cyrus.

"No, but the photo op will be epic," he said, his tone acerbic.

Narrowing her eyes, she focused on the councilman, trying to figure out if he was working with Sebastian.

Eventually, the talk concluded with Edward shooting a sizzling glare Vivian's way. Vivian leaned down to whisper to Marie before she stood up and left the table. Conversation buzzed in the large room while they waited for dessert, and Claire elbowed Cyrus.

"Edward just got up too. Let's follow them," she whispered.

"I'll stay here and keep an eye on the room," Zander murmured.

Nodding, the two of them trailed behind Vivian—slowly, so it appeared they were going to the restroom. Suddenly, she veered right and disappeared through a side door off the bathroom hallway. Claire and Cyrus stopped short, waiting...

And then, as if they'd foreseen it, Edward bolted past them and through the side door.

"Come on," Claire hissed, waving him forward with her hand. "We need to eavesdrop."

She stealthily walked down the hall and gingerly pushed open the door, not wanting to make a sound. Holding her finger over her lips, Cyrus spared her an annoyed glance before nodding. Easing into the stairwell, she gently closed the door and perked her ears.

"You couldn't just leave it alone, Vivian!" Edward yelled, hushed but furious. "I told you, Dr. Petrov is a huge donor. For someone who didn't want a political life, you seem to keep putting your nose in it!"

"Dr. Petrov is a snake who falsified results on two different clinical trials to the FDA. That's a crime, Edward! One that could potentially hurt millions of people, and I won't let that happen. He's going to jail, and screw him and his money!"

"Twenty of his friends have threatened to pull their campaign donations if you testify against him, Viv. Don't you understand? This could ruin me."

"I would think you would be more worried about your soul being ruined! Don't you care he took dirty money from a pharmaceutical company that knew he falsified data? The Edward I loved all those years ago would never accept blood money."

"Everything is a goddamn moral issue with you, Viv. Good god. We were in college then. Of course, I was idealistic. Now, I understand how the world works. It's too bad you're still stuck in this utopian fantasy. It's going to cause you a shit ton of trouble. Mark my words."

Silence echoed off the concrete walls until Vivian said, "Is that a threat?"

Edward let out a ragged sigh. "For god's sake. Don't be ridiculous."

"You're in deep with the Knights of Washington, Edward. It's disgusting. I abhor everything they stand for."

"So do I!" he exclaimed, frustration in his tone. "But I need their money. Don't you understand that once I gain even more power, I can stop them?"

Moments ticked by. Finally, she asked, "You truly believe that, don't you?" Claire heard the warble of tears in her voice. "How can you delude yourself this way? The more you rise to prominence, the more corrupt you will become. Don't you see that?"

"Vivian," he said, compassion entering his voice, "I won't let that happen—"

"Don't touch me!" she interrupted. "I saw this in you, all those years ago. It broke my heart, Edward, but I knew you would always love power more than you would ever love anyone or anything else, including me."

"I did love you, Vivian."

"Not enough. Never enough to disassociate yourself from bad men and choose goodness. It's heartbreaking because I truly think you could've been an amazing public servant. Now, we'll never know."

"I'm sorry you feel that way," he said, his tone low. "I've always tried to show you how much I care. Even when you had Marie with Jonathan and he left, I offered to help support her even though she wasn't mine. I just wanted to help you and your daughter."

"I never needed your money, Edward. That was always so hard for you to understand. I just wanted your love. You use money as a Band-Aid to try and fix everything, but take it from this washed-up physician: Band-Aids are temporary and quite often fall off."

"So what now?"

"I'm going to testify, Edward. You can try and stop me. Hell, you can try and kill me. I see the cars that sit outside our house at night, watching us."

"What are you talking about?"

She scoffed. "You seem genuinely surprised. Maybe you don't even know. Perhaps you're already just a puppet, and they're pulling both our strings. Regardless, I'm taking Dr. Petrov down. Don't ask me to cease again. And for the last time, leave me and Marie alone."

"Vivian—"

"No!" she yelled. "I mean it, Edward. We're done."

Something shuffled, and Claire realized Vivian was walking back toward the hallway door. Gently pushing it open, she grabbed Cyrus and tugged him out. He hobbled on the crutches, his body falling into the wall for support. Hearing the door begin to creak open, Claire grabbed the folds of his sport coat, drew him down, and cemented her lips to his.

The door swung open, and Vivian gasped. "Oh, Claire. Cyrus. Sorry. I, uh...I didn't see you there."

"Sorry," Claire said, her lips buzzing from touching Cyrus's. "I couldn't help it. He looks so good in the suit."

Vivian smiled as she assessed them. "Did either of you, um, hear anything from the stairwell? I went there to get some air."

"Oh, no," Claire said, waving her hand. "I was too busy sucking this one's face. Hope you got a few minutes of relief though."

"I did," she said with a quick tilt of her head. "I need to get back to Marie. See you both inside." She sauntered off, and Claire looked up at Cyrus with wide eyes. "Holy shit! That was close!"

"Sucking face?" he asked, his featured scrunched. "You couldn't do better than that?"

Breathing a laugh, she shrugged. "Sorry. Best I could do in a pinch. Can you believe that conversation though?"

Suddenly, the door burst open again, and Cyrus tugged her into his body, planting another kiss on her mouth. Edward burst through, halting briefly when he saw them and then muttering to himself as he carried on. When he was out of sight, Claire brushed her lips against Cyrus's, loving how smooth yet firm they were.

His rapid intake of air at the gentle touch made her shiver, and she felt a gush of wetness between her thighs.

"Your lips are so soft, Claire," he whispered, the words vibrating against her lips as he barely grazed her.

"I was just thinking the same about you."

He scowled. "Men don't have soft lips. Mine are manly and strong."

"Whatever they are, they're gorgeous." Placing one last peck upon them for good measure, she lowered her heels back to the floor. "That was close."

"But we got the info we needed. Judging by that conversation, Marie isn't Edward's daughter. Also, it seems Edward has no idea Sebastian and his counterparts are trying to alter the future and ensure Vivian and Marie get hurt."

"At least he's not a super-villain. Seems like he might just be a power-hungry guy who fell in with the wrong people. Such a shame."

"It sure is. Come on, let's get back inside." Sliding the crutches under his arms, they began the trek back to the banquet room to update Zander.

Chapter 20

Once the night wound down, they gathered their things, ready to head home. Edward stood by the dining room doors shaking hands with people as they exited. Claire approached him, hand extended.

"Thank you, Councilman Randolph. Your speech was lovely."

As he enfolded her hand, curiosity sparked in his hazel eyes. "Thank you. Have we met before?"

"I don't think so," she said, suddenly feeling nervous. "I'm one of Doc Viv's patients."

"You might have met at the library," a deep voice chimed behind her. Shock pervaded her veins as she turned to find Sebastian limping toward them. Armed by the knowledge she'd created his limp, she straightened her spine, preparing for a confrontation.

"Sebastian," Edward said, removing his hand from Claire's and extending it to him. "I thought you weren't going to make it. Glad you could come, although we're winding down."

"I wouldn't miss this for the world." His cold gaze was glued to Claire. "And who is this pretty little thing?"

Gritting her teeth, Claire said, "This *woman* is one of Dr. Elders' guests."

"Ah, the vibrant Dr. Elders," Sebastian said. "Such a beautiful beacon in our world. I hope her light never gets extinguished." The veiled threat set off warning bells in Claire's brain.

"Sebastian Hawthorne is one of my smartest advisors," Edward said. "He got caught in an unfortunate accident during a home improvement project the other day, so we weren't sure he was going to make it."

"Oh, I hope you're okay?" Claire said, batting her eyelashes as Sebastian glowered at her.

"I'll be fine. Thank you."

"This is Cyrus and Zander. They both really hate unfortunate incidents like that. I'm so lucky to have them by my side so one doesn't befall me."

"I find unfortunate things happen when you least expect them," was his ominous reply.

"Well, this took a turn," Edward said, nervously chuckling. "Claire, it was a pleasure. Cyrus, Zander." He gave them both a courteous tilt of his head. "I'm going to continue to say goodbye to our guests. Sebastian, I'd like you to meet the Remingtons. They almost never venture out in public and are valued contributors to my campaign."

"Of course. Goodbye, Claire. I really hope we meet again soon."

Claire clenched her fist, two seconds away from lodging it in his face. Cyrus grabbed it and laced his fingers through hers, tugging her toward the door.

"Come on, Finch. Not here."

They debriefed in the taxi, discussing Vivian and Edward's argument, before dropping Zander off and heading to their apartment. Exhausted, Claire trailed to the bedroom to undress, frustrated the clasp on her dress wouldn't budge. Opening the bedroom door, she called to Cyrus.

His attempt to unclasp it took some maneuvering, but he finally got it open. Turning to face him, she smiled.

"Thanks. Let me help you too." Lifting her hands to his tie, she began to slide the fabric apart, slowly unknotting it. Desire simmered in his eyes, and she seized the opportunity. Lifting her chin, she licked her lips, loving the resulting flare of arousal in his brown orbs.

"What are you thinking right now?" she whispered.

Heavy breaths exited his lips. "That I'm drained. That fundraiser was pretty stuffy."

She nodded, the fabric of the tie making small wispy sounds as she unknotted it. "You did well on the ankle tonight."

"It's feeling a lot better." The gravel in his voice oscillated through every cell in her body. As she tugged the silk, she noticed his shoulders tense. Claire was certainly no seductress, but she'd read every single erotic novel Lainey's mother had stored on her old e-reader at the hub. They were filled with romance stories of every kind: from immortal vampires who seduced sexy sorceresses to billionaire businessmen who charmed submissive women. In the stories, several of the men had reveled in bondage and submission from their partners. Did Cyrus secretly have those same fantasies?

Realizing there was only one way to find out, she slid the tie from his shirt and began slowly wrapping it around her wrist. A vein pulsed in his neck as his chest heaved.

"What are you doing?"

"I'm binding my wrist."

His irises darted between hers, and she could feel the lust vibrating from his frame.

"It's okay," she whispered, turning and aligning her wrists together behind her back. "Tie them together."

He stood frozen, and she almost took pity on him. Her tall, strong soldier, terrified to show her this part of himself. Glancing at him over her shoulder, she backed into his solid body.

"I'm not the timid wallflower you decided I was somewhere along the way, Cyrus. Tie my hands together. I won't break. There are condoms in the drawer," she said, gesturing to the bedside table with her head.

Warm breath brushed over her ear. "You bought condoms?"

"Uh, yeah," she said, wiggling against him. "After you made me explode in the bathroom, I bought several boxes."

He grunted and remained still, inciting her frustration. Turning around, she let the tie fall to the floor. Reaching behind her neck, she unzipped her dress and pushed it to her knees, stepping out of it on her bare feet. Standing in her bra and panties, she let him look his fill.

"I'll never be skinny like other women you've probably been with," she said, tamping down the urge to cover herself. "But I think you want me anyway, so I'm standing here waiting for you to make love to me, Cyrus. I haven't done this in a long time, and I'm dying for you to touch me."

He stepped forward, sliding his palms to cup her cheeks. "You deserve promises I can't make, Claire."

"I don't want promises. I just want you."

His inner struggle was evident as she reached behind her back and unclasped her bra. Tossing it to the floor, she heard his swift inhale.

"Now, Cyrus. Stop hiding from me. It's time."

His gaze fell to her breasts, caressing them with such fervor her nipples tightened into tight points. Clenching her thighs together, she almost whimpered at the ache deep in her core. Never had time moved so slowly. Offering herself to him, she waited.

His hands tightened on her face before he murmured, "I deluded myself this wouldn't happen."

Feeling her lips curve, she slid her arms around his neck. "I told you, you were toast, chief."

He nuzzled his nose against hers. "Claire?"

"Mm-hmm..."

"I love it when you're right." Pressing his lips to hers, he engulfed her in a blazing kiss.

* * * *

Cyrus consumed Claire's lips, understanding they'd been slowly dancing toward this very point in time for so very long. Every crooked smile. Every moment spent patiently teaching him to read. Every time he'd consoled her as she cried or needed comfort. Each moment a building block that comprised the intricate vise she'd weaved around his heart. So thankful for her tenacious nature, he pulled her close, unable to push her away any longer.

Armed with his newfound acceptance of his burning desire to touch her, he glided his hands down her arms, over the small of her back, and cupped the generous globes of her ass, pulling her into his surging cock. She groaned, digging her nails into his neck as her tongue lavished his, the tiny pricks driving him insane with lust.

His broad hands massaged the sweet mounds, Cyrus almost drowning in disbelief that he was finally caressing her there. Now the dam had broken free, he vowed to unlock every dream he'd ever had about her. Crouching down, he slipped his arm under her knees and lifted her, carrying her to the bed. Gently laying her across the comforter, she grinned up at him, adorable and sly. Strands of her multicolored hair spread across the pillow as her skin flushed beneath his gaze. Locating the discarded tie, he picked it up and returned to her side.

Curious green eyes watched as he lifted her arms above her head. The headboard was solid, meaning he couldn't tie her to it, so he did the next best thing. Pushing her wrists together, he bound them with the tie above her head.

"Leave them there," he commanded softly.

She nodded, squirming on the bed, her large breasts beckoning him as he struggled to breathe. Seeing her like this, bound and waiting, caused something inside to roar, and he reminded himself to take it slow.

"How long since you've done this?"

She bit her lip. "Not since I was seventeen. He was sweet."

Cyrus touched his finger to her collarbone, reveling in her gasp, before trailing it over her soft skin to circle her nipple. Puckered and ready, it seemed to summon him.

"I'm not sure I'm a sweet lover," he said, closing his fingers around the bud and slightly pinching. "But I can try."

She mewled as his fingers twisted her taut skin. "Sweet is overrated," she rasped. "I want you to ravish me."

His fingers tightened upon the tiny nub, rewarding her. "I need complete honesty from you, sweetheart. Tell me what feels good and if you want me to stop at any time. Do you understand?"

The little seductress pushed her breast into his hand, asking for more. "Yes," she breathed.

Stepping back, he removed his clothes, gaze cemented to hers as she softly panted upon the bed. Her eyes grew wide as she observed his cock, proud and erect as it reached for her from the thatch of dark hair between his thighs. Naked, he sauntered toward her, hooking his fingers over the hem of her panties and dragging them off her legs. Deftly climbing over her body, careful not to further strain his ankle, he straddled her. Content to gaze at her beauty for just a moment, he slid his hand between her breasts, loving the sight of his splayed fingers between the generous mounds.

"Cyrus," she whimpered, writhing beneath him.

"I could never compare you to anyone else, Claire. You're the most beautiful woman I've ever seen."

Tears shined in her eyes as her chin slightly quivered. "I never believed that until you."

Lowering his body, he placed soft kisses on her reddened cheeks and button nose. "So fucking beautiful," he whispered, trailing his lips down her neck, loving her resulting high-pitched mewl as he traveled to her breast. Rimming it with his lips, he gazed at her.

Passion laced her expression as he sucked her into his mouth, spreading wetness all over the taut nub before tugging it between his teeth. Her body arched under his, the soft skin of her thigh rubbing against his shaft, and he closed his eyes in ecstasy. Lowering his hand, he pushed her thigh away and glided his hand to her core as his tongue played with her nipple. Finding her wet and ready, the springy curls drenched as they tickled his hand, he circled her taut opening with his finger.

"Oh, god," she moaned, pushing into his hand, her body begging him for more. Granting the request, he slipped his finger inside her tight channel, feeling her muscles push back against the invasion.

"Open that sweet little body for me," he said, maintaining her gaze as his lips trailed butterfly kisses down her abdomen. He stopped to dip his tongue in her navel, dying to taste every inch of her, before making his way to her mound. Sliding his palms over her inner thighs, he pushed them apart, forcing the sides of her knees against the mattress, opening her to his heated gaze. The wet, swollen folds of her pussy glistened back at him as saliva pooled in his mouth. Touching his finger to her curls, the corner of his mouth lifted.

"Brown."

"So boring," she said, grinning at him shyly. "You'll only see that color there. I need more variety up top."

Lowering his face, he buried it in the curls, reveling in the scratchy softness against his chin. Pulling her folds apart, he extended his tongue and licked her, from the sensitive skin behind her opening, over the drenched hole, and up to the sensitive bud. Tossing her head back on the pillow, her body fell limp below him.

"*Ohmygod*," she moaned, pushing her mound against him. "More."

He played with her...licking...nipping...teasing her to see what she liked best. Every so often, she would close those gorgeous legs around his head, causing him to push her thighs apart and pin her to the bed. The dominant action sated some deep-seated impulse in his soul as she writhed below him. Her willingness to let him bind her and hold her open while he drank her essence was intoxicating.

Needing to connect with her, he softly commanded, "Look at me, Claire."

Hooded green eyes latched onto him, and he drew apart the sensitive skin of her opening. Extending his tongue, he impaled her, surging inside before drawing back and entering yet again. She whimpered his name as he fucked her with his tongue, showing her that this was only the beginning. Now that he'd tasted her, he was dead set on executing every single fantasy he'd ever had. God, there were so many things he longed to do to her body.

His shaft jerked, reminding him it was ready to claim her. "I promise I'm going to make you come this way soon, but I want to be inside you the first time you go over the edge, honey."

Her eyes lit with excitement. "Yes. I want that too."

With one last soft peck to her mound, he reached over and pulled open the drawer. Laughter leaped from his throat when he saw the multiple boxes of condoms. "You have a lot of faith in this old man, Claire."

"You can do it, chief. I believe in you."

Chuckling, he opened the box and tore off one of the packets. Rolling the condom over his erection, he grinned at her.

"You're staring, Finch."

"I'm anticipating getting pounded like one of the heroines in Mara's novels. Bring it on."

Sliding over her, he chuckled and shook his head. "Stop making me laugh. I'm supposed to be all sexy and brooding, right?"

"You brood enough," she said, winking. "You can laugh a little bit. It won't kill you."

Balancing on his knees, he lifted her ankle and rested it on his shoulder before doing the same with the other. Palming her shins, he caressed them as he stared down at her.

"Look at you," he whispered.

She lay before him, arms bound above her head, those magnificent breasts above the flare of her hips. Reaching for his shaft, he guided the tip to her core, hissing at the sensitive connection even through the condom. Gripping her legs tight against his chest, he began to nudge inside.

Her hips surged toward his, her swollen folds dragging him inside until he closed his eyes, inhaling a deep breath to steady himself. Lifting his lids, he stared into her desire-laden irises as he began to pump his hips. The tight tissues of her swollen channel choked him, squeezing his cock in a constricted fist of pleasure. Licking his thumb, he ensured it was wet before lowering it to her clit. Increasing the thrust of his hips, he began to circle the sensitive bud.

"That feels so good," she whispered, her head tossing back on the pillow.

He growled in response, surging inside her as his balls tightened. Her breasts bobbled as her body moved beneath him, limp and open. Soft curves led to dips and hollows he found so achingly beautiful as he plunged deep within. Kissing her leg, he buried his face against it, wanting to hold every part of her close as he loved her. Feeling her body tense beneath him, he increased the pressure on her clit.

A deep-throated moan escaped her lips as her body arched beneath him. Screaming his name, she began to come, the silken walls of her core milking his cock as she exploded. Reduced to ragged nerve endings, every ounce of his skin tingled as his orgasm loomed on the horizon.

Sliding his arms behind her knees, he stretched over her, pushing her legs high as he balanced on his palms. As she shuddered below him, he called her name. Gorgeous eyes brimming with sated lust and emotion stared back, deep into his soul. It was the most intimate connection he'd ever experienced while making love, and his pounding heart slammed inside his chest. Capturing her lips in a simmering kiss, he fell over the edge, jetting his release into her body as she quaked below him. Euphoria overtook him as he depleted every drop. Unable to balance, he collapsed over her, burying his face in her neck as he made sure to keep his full weight from crushing her. Gasps blanketed the room as they struggled to catch their breath.

Her laughter encircled his sweaty skin, full of bliss. "Can I move my arms now?"

The submissive question elicited a growl from deep within. "Mm-hmm. Slip them over my head and hold me while I recover," he murmured into her neck.

"Aw," she said, following his directive. "You want me to hold you. That's super cute."

His lids closed, pressed together in firm joy, as her body surrounded him. "I always want you to hold me, sweetheart."

She shivered at the words and relaxed beneath him. The trust she displayed shifted age-old doubts deep within about concepts he'd considered closed ages ago. If she could bestow such trust and openness upon him, couldn't he at least contemplate the possibility of building something more permanent with her? Perhaps having kids and creating a family? Unsure of the answer, he snuggled into her, pushing it away for later so he could enjoy the moment.

Eventually, he pulled from her tight grip and hobbled to the bathroom to dispose of the condom. When he returned, she held her bound hands up to him.

"Untie me."

His actions were meticulous but deft as he gazed down at her, dragging the loosened silk across her still-turgid nipples before letting it fall to the floor. Extending her arms, she reached for him, giving him one of her glorious, crooked smiles. Falling into her embrace, he pulled her close, stroking her hair as she sighed into his chest.

"Finally," she mumbled against his pec.

He grinned against her hair. "Finally," he said softly.

Content and sated, they stroked each other as they silently contemplated how things had irrevocably changed.

Chapter 21

The next morning, Claire awoke, Cyrus's warm body next to her. His constant, stable breathing gave her a sense of peace in this world where they didn't quite belong. Yet, knowing they fit together in this new, passionate bond filled her with such purpose. Determined to take advantage of his ability to let down his walls, she vowed not to squander the opportunity.

He teased her when he awoke, telling her she still looked beautiful even with the mussed strands of her hair that extended in various directions, and she playfully slapped him on the chest before rolling out of bed to cook them breakfast. That first meal together after they'd finally made love was possibly the happiest moment of her life thus far.

Claire threw herself into researching the Knights of Washington, determined to figure out why Sebastian was digging for information on Marie now that they were pretty sure Marie wasn't Edward's daughter. Cyrus and Zander worked alongside her, Cyrus's ankle healing nicely. He ditched the crutches soon after the fundraiser, teasing Claire that this would make him even more proficient in the bedroom. As far as she was concerned, he was already a rock star.

Although she had limited experience, she found Cyrus's lovemaking to be a potent combination of tender and possessive, reverent and assertive. Never had she felt so cherished as when he stared into her eyes when he was inside her deepest place. She'd already been in love with him before their relationship turned romantic. Now, she'd fallen so far she couldn't even dream of a life without him by her side, as her partner and the father of her children. The desire to achieve those dreams burned so deeply within her soul, and she was determined to help him shed his reservations so they could build a life together.

One morning, a few days after they'd first made love, she awoke. Resting her head on her elbow, she traced his face as he slept. Eventually, his features contorted, and he batted her hand away.

"Leave me alone, woman," he mumbled, eyes still closed. "You wore me out."

She glided her thigh over his, spurring him to lift his lids and shoot her a droll look.

"Aaaaaand now, I'm awake," he teased.

Claire chuckled as she assessed him. Wanting to tread carefully, she decided to dip her toe into the water of the many extremely important topics they needed to discuss if they were going to have the future she so desperately wanted with him.

"Tell me the story about what happened with Dalton," she said, sensing his muscles tense. "Please be open with me. I truly want to understand what happened. We've never really discussed it at length."

"I don't want to discuss it with you, Claire."

"Why? I don't hold any part of myself back from you, Cyrus. It hurts when you close yourself off to me."

"Sweetheart," he whispered, running his fingers through the hair at her temple, "I'm so thankful Lewis brought you to the hub and shielded you from the war. Being a soldier in that world could rip a person's soul apart if you let it. It hardened me, and I question whether I lost something along the way. A part of my humanity or something. I sometimes wonder if what happened with Dalton proved I'd crossed a moral line from which I couldn't return."

"Tell me," she whispered. "Please."

Sighing, he took her hand, placing a kiss on her palm before resting it over his heart. The organ thumped with several firm pulses before he finally spoke. With his deep baritone, he recounted the fateful experience. Dalton had shown his true colors with Lainey and been outed as a traitor, and Lewis had tasked Cyrus with transporting him to Solera, where he would be turned over for trial. A few miles into their journey, Dalton began to struggle against his restraints. When Cyrus tried to stop him, the man had grabbed the knife from Cyrus's belt, causing him to pull his gun and shoot.

"I should've aimed for his leg or shoulder," Cyrus said, staring ahead as he appeared lost in the memories. "But I shot him in the heart. He died instantly. Even though he was a traitor and a spy, he deserved due process. In the heat of the moment, I denied him that. I have no idea how to reconcile it."

"You acted in self-defense," she said, rubbing her palm over his chest.

"Yes, it's what I tell myself to justify it, but I'm just not sure it's an acceptable excuse," he said, gazing at her as guilt swam in his eyes. "When faced with a moment where I had to make a split-second decision, I went for the kill. What does that say about me?"

"That you wanted to live. That's not evil, Cyrus. It's just human."

His slow intake of breath was ragged as he slid his hand over hers. "Maybe. How can I guarantee I won't make another disastrous mistake like that?"

"You can't," she said, shrugging. "We all make mistakes, and sometimes, they're pretty awful. It was a really terrible outcome, but you're still here. You have the opportunity to strive to do good every day. You've done so much to protect each one of us. I hope you'll give yourself credit for that."

"I couldn't even prevent you from getting kidnapped." His brow formed a slight frown. "So I'm not sure how great I am at safeguarding you."

"Well, I saved myself from that situation, thank you very much. But I'm so grateful you're here with me, Cyrus. I feel so safe with you."

"I'm glad."

Glancing at the ceiling, she contemplated. "I understand your reservations, but you can also take what you learned from the experience with Dalton and let the remorse drive you to make an impact. Lessons from those terrible moments in our lives are always the most important, aren't they?"

His brows lifted as he pondered. "I guess they are, in a way."

"Mistakes are inevitable when you're human, but the future is ours to decide."

"I appreciate your optimism, Finch. It's one of the things I admire most about you."

"I am pretty optimistic," she said, pursing her lips. "And I'm also pretty badass in this timeline. Holy crap, Cyrus. I feel like a whole new person here."

"Yeah?"

Nodding, she wistfully began naming all the things that were so amazing about their current timeline. The unlimited hair dye, technology at their fingertips, and the endless food.

"But more than that, I've found a strength here I didn't know I possessed. I was pretty sheltered at the hub and relied on you and the others to protect me. I met so few people that I talked to the chickens sometimes." Snickering, she bit her lip. "I *think* they tried to talk back."

His chest vibrated as he chuckled.

"When I think about how far I've come…I mean, look at what happened with Sebastian. I was naïve as hell when he first approached me, and only weeks later, I'm pretty sure I knocked him down a testicle, slimy bastard. I've gained this whole new confidence, especially when you look at me like you are right now." Running her thumb over his bottom lip, she shivered. "God, Cyrus, I feel like Black Widow or Superwoman from Lewis's old comics. Strong and pretty and fierce."

"You're all of those things, sweetheart. I always saw that in you."

Love swished through her frame at the sentimental words. "I freaking love it here. I don't know if Lainey's coming to get us, but at this point, I'm not sure I'd go with her."

Chuckling, he arched a brow. "You were born a few decades too late."

"Yep. This era is my jam. I love it."

"I'm glad you're happy."

"I'm so happy," she whispered.

When they'd loved each other once more, they arose to start the day. Claire deemed their conversation constructive and decided she would keep chipping away at his reservations, hoping he would be able to overcome them and build a life with her. Content to take it day by day, she kept the faith their newfound love would prevail.

* * * *

"At this point, I think we've uncovered the bulk of what we're looking for," Zander said from his seat at the round table in the corner of his office.

Hundreds of pages of research lined the table, each filled with information on the Knights of Washington's most prominent members. They were mostly rich old men who were on the record as staunch proponents of suppressing the poor and underserved and supporting candidates who would reflect their views. For all their research on Edward Randolph, they hadn't come up with anything quite so cut and dry. Instead, he seemed to be a young, eager candidate who had risen to prominence with their donations, and now, several years later, was beholden to their wishes if he wanted the contributions to keep flowing.

Sebastian, on the other hand, was an anomaly. He'd appeared on the scene two years ago, showing up for one of the Knights' gatherings at the meeting hall. Although he had documentation—a traceable social security

121

number, tax returns, and a previous address history—it all seemed a bit too "neat."

"You can create a documented history pretty easily," Zander said, trailing his finger over one of the reports they'd run on Sebastian. "I'd already researched him before his run-in with you in the library."

Claire's eyes narrowed. "How do you create an entire history you never lived?"

Zander shrugged. "You steal a dead person's social security number. Someone without a family who dies in a nursing home. Then, you falsify old phone and utility bills to create an address history. It's pretty seamless, and if no one cares to look too closely, you can get away with it indefinitely."

"Wow," Claire said, puffing a breath through her lips. "Good to know in case we're stuck here."

Cyrus's brows lifted. "Let's hope it doesn't come to that, but, yes, it's rather interesting that one can create a life from nothing. Makes you wonder if anything is truly real in this world."

"So we've uncovered the information. Now, we need to figure out what to do with it. From what I can tell, Sebastian is the outlier in the group, which makes sense considering he most likely time traveled here like we did."

Zander shook his head and muttered, "Still so weird."

"At this point, I think we can logically conclude he's working alone with one subordinate, Michael Lowe, whom we've identified as the man inside the van when he abducted me."

"Yes," Zander said. "Michael seems to be a zealot Sebastian recruited because of his desire to join the Knights of Washington. He wasn't rich or connected, so they wouldn't initially accept him, but Sebastian gained his allegiance. In return, he convinced the Knights to induct him."

"So who's Sebastian working for? Victor Hernandez?"

"That would be the logical answer," Cyrus said, rubbing his chin. "I mean, as far as 'logical' goes when you're discussing something like a nefarious enemy sent back by a future leader of an evil regime."

"Good point," Zander said.

"Okay, so Sebastian wants to ensure Marie is harmed, and, supposedly, I'm going to save her. So badass," Claire said, patting herself on the back and grinning.

"I've been staking the black sedan that's parked outside of Vivian's house each night," Zander said. "It seems Michael is doing the surveillance, although he always wears a baseball cap, and the pictures are dark, so I can't be sure. Luckily, Vivian lives above the clinic, and it's an extremely high-trafficked area, both by her patients and by cops. It would be really stupid for them to attack her there."

"Should we approach her and warn her that someone might be trying to harm Marie?" Cyrus asked.

"She's aware someone's surveilling her, according to her conversation with Edward," Claire said. "Doc Viv is pretty sharp. I say we keep things the way they are for now. Zander can keep watch over her house at night, and we'll do some reconnaissance on the old dudes who make up the Knights. Maybe we can find a way to get Sebastian excommunicated from the group by blackmailing one of the members to blacklist him or something. If he loses access to Edward, his mission will be severely hindered."

"I'm good with that," Zander said, standing and stacking some of the papers. "I don't like that this creep is stalking Doc Viv and want to keep an eye on her anyway. The work she does to help patients is really altruistic, and she seems to just do it out of the goodness of her heart. Not many people like her around, and I'd like to make sure she's safe."

Claire shot a glance at Cyrus and waggled her eyebrows. She'd told him she suspected Zander had a thing for Doc Viv, and his desire to keep her safe only added to that theory. Cyrus winked at her, acknowledging the sentiment.

Armed with their respective duties, the members of **Montgomery, Finch and Katz, π's for Hire** got to work. Claire's partners didn't seem to find the name nearly as hilarious and cheeky as she did, but, honestly, she didn't give a damn. Deciding it was awesome and they had absolutely no sense of humor, she declared it official and binding, much to their amused chagrin.

Chapter 22

Zander Katz sat in his navy hatchback on the darkened street, warily eyeing the black sedan half a block away. The man inside observed Vivian each night once the sun set, causing Zander to worry. As he'd pointed out to Claire and Cyrus, she was an amazing woman, and he definitely didn't want anything to happen to her, all because of a relationship with Edward Randolph that she'd ended years ago.

Also, she was smart as hell and quite easy on the eyes. Claire had informed him she didn't date, which he thought was a terrible shame. Someone like her, who worked so hard to care for others, should be cherished. Of course, Marie was a source of affection for her, but Zander found himself wishing she had a partner; someone who could hold her after a long day and caress her wavy brown hair as she sought solace in his arms. Someone who offered her comfort after she returned inside from the long minutes she spent outside at dusk, lifting her face to the newly risen moon, eyes closed, as she inhaled the spring air. It must've been some new-age yoga breathing thing Zander didn't even begin to understand, but it seemed to bring her peace. Still, he felt she deserved to return inside to a loving embrace—one that consoled and supported her...

Scowling, he acknowledged he was imagining himself as that partner. Him, a divorcé who'd failed so drastically at his first marriage. He hadn't spoken to his ex-wife in several years and expected it to stay that way. Since they had no children, there was no reason to stay in touch. They'd grown apart over their five-year marriage while he'd built his P.I. business and she'd plowed through law school, and one day, they'd looked at each other and realized they were strangers.

He'd had several one-night stands in the years since the divorce, but that was all he'd even cared to contemplate. Telling himself he just wasn't the relationship type, he focused on his business and pleasured himself to a fair amount of porn—when his slow as hell internet wasn't buffering. Which made it that much stranger that he was having these thoughts about

Vivian. Imagining holding her and staring into her dark green eyes as he caressed her slightly freckled skin. Quite strange indeed.

A vicious knock on the car window dragged him from his musings, causing him to jump and almost spill the lukewarm coffee he was holding. Turning to find a furious Vivian Elders, he rolled down the window.

"Would you like to tell me why you're staking out my house?" she asked, hands on her hips, her features contorted in a mask of annoyance. "It's enough that the idiot in the black car doesn't think I'm onto him,"—she gestured to the black sedan—"but you too? I assure you, I know every cop in this neighborhood, and they'll be here in thirty seconds if I call them."

"I'm sorry," he said, feeling like a scolded child. "I wanted to keep an eye on him." He jerked his head toward Michael's car. "Didn't like the thought of you being watched."

"So you're watching the guy who's watching me?" Lifting her hands, she gave an exasperated huff. "That's absurd. You know, I thought you were one of the good guys when Claire and Cyrus introduced me to you. They're shady as hell, and I think there's a lot more to their story, but they still seem like good people."

Setting the cup in the holder, Zander reached for the handle and slightly opened the door. Vivian slapped her hands against it, shooting him a glare. "Why are you getting out?"

"Because I want to speak to you eye to eye," he said, doing his best to appear genuine. "I'd really like to explain why I'm here."

Her eyes narrowed as she sized him up before stepping back. Rising from the car, he shut the door behind him and leaned on it. Pulling a pack of cigarettes from his pocket, he brought one to his lips and reached for his lighter. Vivian plucked the smoke from his mouth and threw it on the ground before stomping on it.

"You're really going to smoke in front of a doctor who treats emphysema patients every day? Not on my watch."

His lips quirked as he admired her spunk. "Sorry," he muttered.

"Well," she said, crossing her arms and tapping her foot. "Go on. I'd love to hear this magnificent explanation of why you're spying on me. I'm all ears."

His eyes roved over her, cheeks reddened and eyes lit with anger, and he realized he was smitten. Damn, but she was a force to be reckoned with.

"Claire, Cyrus and I think you might be in danger. That idiot over there," he said, cocking his head toward Michael's car, "is surveilling you, but he's not the brightest bulb in the socket." Zander tapped his temple with his finger. "I'd really like to tell you more, but it's probably safer if we go inside."

She scoffed. "You think I'm going to invite you inside my house? Where my daughter is sleeping?"

Realizing he had nothing to lose, he went for the gold. "Yes, ma'am. I think you are. And if you're open to it, I think we could brew a pot of coffee, and I could tell you why I think you're in danger."

Her eyes grew wide, and she seemed a bit stunned.

"We know about your connection to Edward Randolph. I'd like to tell you more, but not out here."

Her nostrils flared. "What connection?"

"We know you dated him in college and that he tried to help support Marie financially even though she isn't his daughter."

The tension slightly eased from her muscles, and he rushed to reassure her. "I'm not here to hurt you, Vivian."

Inhaling deeply, she nodded. "Come on." Waving him forward, he fell into step behind her as she trailed to the house. "I only have decaf, so that'll have to do."

"Sounds good."

As she walked down the sidewalk, she flipped the bird toward the black sedan. "Fucking asshole. I keep giving the cops his license plate number, and he just rents a new car. They're all over it though. They patrol the street every five minutes. I don't know why he wastes his time."

Zander's lips curved as he followed her up the stairs, through the clinic, and then up to the second-floor kitchen where she made them coffee. One cup turned into two...which turned into three as he updated her on the Knights of Washington. She knew some of the details already and apprised him of her plans to testify against Dr. Petrov, who was a high-ranking member of the Knights. He decided not to tell her about the whole time travel aspect of things—hell, he still barely believed it himself—but he made sure to impart everything else he knew. Finally, well past two a.m., she walked him to the front door.

"Thanks for detailing me. I assure you, I feel safe. Lawrence, the police chief for the local precinct, makes sure I'm protected. I treat a lot of people in this neighborhood, and he reciprocates in kind."

"I'm glad to know that, but don't be surprised if you see me outside anyway. I want to make sure you're safe, Vivian, and Marie too."

"Thank you." His gaze fell to her neck, which bobbled slightly as she swallowed. "I don't want you to feel obligated—"

"No obligation," he cut in, lifting his hand to brush away the wavy tuft of hair that had fallen over her brow.

She emitted a soft gasp, straightening as she assessed him.

"I'm sorry," he said, dropping his hand. "That was really presumptuous. I usually don't go around touching women who don't want it. Have a good night, Vivian. I'll do my best to keep you safe." With a nod, he stepped onto the front porch and began trailing down the stairs before she called his name.

"Yeah?" he asked, turning back.

"I didn't say I didn't want you to touch me. It was actually...quite nice." With a tilt of her head, she gave him a soft grin and shut the door.

Zander turned around, a huge smile overtaking his lips. Filled with a newfound energy, he all but skipped back to the car, noticing the black sedan was nowhere to be found.

Chapter 23

Claire and Cyrus spent several days tracking the senior members of the Knights of Washington. Eventually, they decided they would target Randall Epstein, a married man who had a nasty habit of hiring expensive escorts several times per week. Claire reveled in the spy work—taking pictures of him with the women, following him to the hotel, tracing his every step. Cyrus, who was now off the crutches but still not particularly mobile, wasn't so enamored with the grunt work, but he worked by her side without complaint. She knew it was because he wanted to protect her, which made her heart melt in a hundred different ways.

They finally confronted Randall in his office. As a Vice President of a local bank in Washington D.C., he was nothing if not punctual. Every morning, at eight a.m. sharp, he pulled up in his black Mercedes, strolled through the bank parking lot and into his office. One morning, Claire observed him park and walked toward him, photographs in hand. Head down, she bumped into him, sending the photographs scattering to the ground.

"Oh, I'm so clumsy. Excuse me, sir," she said, crouching down. "Would you mind helping me?"

Randall seemed annoyed but bent down and began helping her stack the photographs. In short order, he understood that he'd been had. Claire heard his gasp as he held one of the images, staring at it with a look of horror on his face.

"Yeah, I think that was Cinnamon. Or was it Cherry? There are so many, I can't keep them straight." Gathering the photos, she stood. "There are multiple copies in several locations, and my bodyguard is right there." She gestured with her head toward Cyrus, who gave a salute as he stood by the back corner of the bank. "It would be best if you bring me into your office so we can discuss there."

"Who are you?" he asked, eyes narrowed.

"I won't discuss details here. In your office, or we send the pictures to your wife and the local media. It's up to you, Randall."

He sized her up, Claire's heart pounding wildly the entire time, before angrily nodding and leading her inside. She sat in one of the leather chairs that faced his desk, while he sat down behind it and scowled.

"Okay, you have my attention. What do you want?"

"I have no desire to give these pictures to your wife, Randall, but that decision depends entirely on you."

"I'm listening," he said as a muscle ticked in his jaw.

"I understand you're heavily involved with the Knights of Washington." After a few moments, she said, "I'll take your silence as confirmation. I'm only interested in one thing. Why are you trying to hurt Vivian Elders' daughter, and how is Sebastian Hawthorne involved?"

"This is absurd—"

"One moment, please," she said, lifting her phone to her ear. "Please release the photos to the media."

"Wait!" Randall said, running his hand over his face. "Okay, I'll tell you what you want to know."

"Hold on. He seems to want to cooperate. I'll call you back." She flipped the phone closed and lifted her brows. "You were saying?"

He leaned back in his chair and steepled his fingers. "There are some members of the Knights who believe Marie is actually Edward's daughter."

"I've overheard conversations that would indicate otherwise."

Randall scoffed. "And you'd believe the words of a whore who helps degenerates and drug dealers for a living?"

Rage welled in her chest, and she told herself to remain calm. "Vivian is my friend, and I expect her to be spoken of with respect. What makes you think Marie is Edward's daughter?"

"The timing of the birth is suspicious. She was only with Jonathan Reeves for eight months before Marie was born."

Claire digested the information. "Maybe they began their affair earlier than anyone thought."

"Perhaps," he said. "The only way we can know for sure is to get a DNA sample from the child. Sebastian hired Zander Katz to perform that very task, but he soon turned against us. Still, Sebastian has assured us he will get the sample, one way or the other. Since Vivian is a physician, she is an expert on making it difficult for us to obtain the DNA we need. There are no cups left behind in public trash cans or any other toss-away items average people would leave behind. At the recent fundraiser, Sebastian told me Vivian ensured her daughter's soda straws were stuffed in her purse after use. Although she's worthless, she is cunning. We've realized we're going to have to find other methods."

"Why do you care if Marie is Edward's daughter?"

"Because Vivian is obsessed with testifying against Dr. Petrov, who is one of our most esteemed patrons. That's bad enough on its own, but if it's found out that Petrov was brought down by the mother of Edward's illegitimate child, it would end his political career. We've invested far too much money in the Randolph brand for it to fail now. It would take years to cultivate someone else. We'd rather ensure we can protect our current candidate."

"He's just a puppet to you," she whispered.

"All politicians are puppets to powerful men. How can you not understand that? My god, you still think the country is run by the people. That it's a democracy. How can you be so blind? One day, that optimism will destroy the entire structure of humanity as we know it."

Claire shivered, realizing the man couldn't begin to understand how true his words really were. "So you're willing to hurt Vivian and Marie just to determine if she's Edward's daughter?"

"Yes," he said. "And if she is, we'll take care of them both. I know this is hard to understand, but they are insignificant nuisances. If they need to be eliminated, they will be."

Claire could barely believe his flippant tone. "Don't you care that you would be murdering two innocent people?"

"A whore and her brat? Not in the least."

Repulsed, Claire stood and scattered the photographs on the floor. Randall surged from behind his desk, his face an angry mask.

"I wouldn't touch her," a deep baritone said from the doorway. "Or I'll snap your neck so fast your head will land in the parking lot."

Relief coursed through Claire, safe in the knowledge Cyrus had her back. "Good luck picking them all up," she said, waving her hand over the photos that now lined the floor. "The teller always gets in at 8:07 a.m. on the dot. Looks like you've got a few minutes left to tuck these away in a drawer. Remember, we have plenty of copies. I don't want to see Sebastian Hawthorne or Michael Lowe within a hundred *miles* of Vivian or Marie. Got it?"

Glowering up at her, he remained silent.

"Your association with Sebastian ends today, Randall. I look forward to your compliance and hope I never have to share those pictures." Giving him a disgusted tilt of her head, she exited the office, Cyrus on her tail.

They walked in silence as she digested the information. "You heard everything?" she asked, glancing up at Cyrus.

"Yes."

Puffing out a breath, she ran her hand through her hair. "We can't let them kill Doc Viv or Marie."

"No one's killing anyone," he said, sliding his arm over her shoulder and pulling her close. "The three of us are on it. Plus, Zander's been watching her nonstop. He's committed to protecting her."

"It so cute," she said, wrinkling her nose. "I hope they end up together."

"That's very romantic," he agreed, squeezing her.

"We'll head to Zander's office at ten to update him on the meeting. Until then, want me to make breakfast? I have some eggs in the fridge."

"I'll never turn down a meal," he said, placing a kiss on her head. "You should've already figured that out."

Glancing down, she squinted at his ankle. "You're walking really well. How's it feeling?"

"Good. I'm just so glad to be off the crutches."

"Yeah, you've been so much better in bed." She snickered at his glower from her teasing. "What? You're just more agile. It's awesome."

"Great. Now I have a complex."

She slid her arm around his waist, always so happy to be in his embrace. When they eventually crossed the threshold of their apartment, Cyrus lifted her over his shoulder and carried her to the bedroom as she giggled.

"What are you doing?"

"Shedding my complex," he said, tossing her on the bed. Claire spent the next hour paying for her comments...and, oh, what magnificent punishment it was.

* * * *

"So that's everything we learned from Randall," Claire said later that morning as they all sat in Zander's office. "The Knights seem to have it out for Vivian and Marie. Although the police are protective of her, and you're keeping an eye out for her, it worries me. How do we get them off her tail?"

"I'm not sure," Zander said, lips pressed together as he mulled the possibilities. "We can turn Sebastian over to the authorities, but the Knights are so connected I'm afraid they'll just ensure he gets free."

"We need to catch him on video trying to break into her property or harm her. The threat of video documentation seems to scare these jerks. They seem to like hiding in the shadows."

"I'll make sure I have my video camera when I keep watch over her house," Zander said.

"Good. We'll also help you surveil," Claire said, standing and wiping her hands on her thighs. "We'll buy a video camera at Radio Shack and try to get some footage of him as well. The ultimate goal is to take him down so he's no longer a threat."

They all agreed, and Claire and Cyrus headed to the electronics store to purchase the video camera. Once home, while she was sitting on the carpeted floor of the living room testing it out, Cyrus sat beside her. Covering her hands as they fiddled with the camera, he said, "We need to talk, Claire."

"Yikes," she said, slowly lowering the camera as her heart began to pound. "That sounds serious. Am I going to like where this is going?"

He smiled, soft and a bit sad. "Claire," he whispered, tucking a strand of hair behind her ear, "these weeks with you have been amazing."

"But...?"

Sighing, he ran his hand over his face. "But we have to accept reality, sweetheart. Lainey isn't coming for us. Eventually, we're going to run out of cash. We need to get jobs and begin to establish our lives here. Zander can help us build identities so we can begin to put down roots."

"Put down roots together, right?" Fear that he was going to leave her began to burrow deep within. "I want to put down roots with you, Cyrus."

His irises darted between hers. "I care about you so much, Claire." A tear trailed down her cheek, and he swiped it with his thumb. "But there are so many obstacles to us building a life together. I just don't think you've really considered them."

"I won't let you go," she said, shaking her head. "I know we can figure out how to make this work."

Sitting back, he lifted his knees and rested his arms over them, blowing out a breath. "I'm forty-three, sweetheart. That's pretty late to start having kids, which is something I've never really been focused on. I'm not against it, but it's a huge decision. I know you want them so badly."

"You'd be such a great dad," she said. "And our kids would be so beautiful."

"Our kids would be Black, Claire. I don't think you've really thought about that and what it means in this timeline. I'm proud of who I am—I always have been—but biracial kids have a whole host of extra challenges."

Puffing out a breath, she nodded. "It would be difficult, for sure. They'll always be straddling two cultures. It's daunting, especially in a world we don't understand ourselves."

Nodding, his eyebrows drew together. "Creating an interracial family in a new timeline is a big decision. It's something I want you to really think about."

Claire chewed her lip as she processed his words. "I will, although I should probably tell you, I've already imagined what our kids would look like in my head a million times."

His lips curved, and emotion entered his gaze, spurring hope deep in her heart.

"We'd have to navigate through the hard times together, but we've done a pretty great job of that so far. I feel like I can accomplish anything with you as my partner, Cyrus."

"We know the future," he said, slowly shaking his head. "Humanity as we know it is going to drastically change on September 4, 2035. How can we bring kids into the world knowing that?"

Claire's chin lifted. "Lainey will succeed. Now that she got the Sphere to work, she'll dedicate all her efforts to stopping Randolph."

"What if she didn't make it to 2035? I appreciate your optimism, but we always knew the chances of defeating Randolph were slim even if everything went according to plan."

"Well, we're armed with more knowledge than most. When September 2035 arrives, we'll make sure our family is protected. We can build a bunker and live there until everything settles. As long as I'm with you, I don't give a damn, Cyrus."

Sighing, he rubbed his hand over his head. "You've always admired my practicality. I'm just trying to be realistic here, honey."

"I'm the first to admit that life is tough, and I don't expect it to get any easier. But if there's one thing I know deep within, it's that I need you by my side." Sliding over the carpet, she pushed his legs down and straddled his thighs. Cupping his face, she stared into his soul. "I love you," she whispered, his features blurring through her tears. "I know you've figured that out, chief."

"Claire," he whispered, palming her cheeks and placing a sweet kiss on her lips. "You're barely thirty years old. Don't you want to experience new things? Explore this new world we landed in? I've lived so much more life than you."

"The age difference has never bothered me," she said, tenderly rubbing his smooth skin. "I think the heart just wants what it wants."

His eyed darted between hers. "I just wonder if you'll wake up one day and realize I'm too old for you or that we're too different."

"I'm scared too, Cyrus. That you'll eventually decide I'm unattractive, and that you can do better—"

"Damn it, Claire. Enough with that stuff. You're gorgeous."

"See? We both have doubts—that's only human. But I'm too afraid to live without you to let them win."

His brow furrowed as he contemplated.

"I need you to choose me, Cyrus. Sooner rather than later would be nice because I'd really like to start our lives together."

His lips twitched. "You're relentless."

Nodding, she wrapped her legs around his waist, shimmying her crotch over his as he pulled her close. "Damn straight," she whispered, softly pecking his lips. "You're going to ask me to marry you, and we're going to have a family. It's a foregone conclusion. Get in line, soldier."

Holding her tight, Cyrus pushed from the floor, anchoring on his good leg.

"Don't hurt your ankle—" she squealed.

"Hush, woman," he said, carrying her to the bed and gently tossing her on top of the comforter.

"Oh, I forgot to tell you," she said, smiling up at him. "I thought of a new word of the day."

Lowering over her, he balanced on his palms, one on each side of her head, as he grinned. "What is it?"

"Venerate." Gliding her hand across his firm jaw, she slid her thumb over his lip. "It means to adore or revere someone."

"Venerate," he whispered. "I venerate you, Claire." Emotion swam in his eyes as he covered her lips with his.

Losing herself to his ardent kisses, she repeated the words of love, unwilling to hold them back any longer...clutching onto hope that he was closer than ever to accepting them.

* * * *

Claire worked with Zander on multiple projects, the two most important being protecting Vivian and Marie, and creating a paper trail for her and Cyrus so they could get jobs. Working with the private investigator was fulfilling, and Claire realized she was pretty fantastic at sleuthing. One day, as she sat in front of the extra computer Zander had purchased for her to use at the office, she floated her idea toward him.

"I want you to hire me as an investigator," she said in a confident tone. "I'm great with research, meticulous with cataloging information, and really enjoy it. I've explored obtaining a private investigator license in D.C., and the GED documentation I've created is sufficient as long as I have an offer of employment from a licensed private detective agency in the district. That's where you come in."

Zander just stared at her, eyebrow arched.

"I know this might seem strange, but I have to get a job sometime and might as well get the ball rolling."

He held up a hand, a huge grin crossing his face. "You're saying this as if you expect me to argue. Honestly, I could use the help, Claire. I've turned down a number of jobs over the past year because I'm only a one-man operation. Having an associate would be really helpful."

"Associate on the partner track," she said, lifting a finger. "After all, I'll be leaving the very successful firm of **Montgomery and Finch, π's for Hire** to join you. It's a real downgrade," she teased.

"Partner track it is," he said, standing and walking over to shake her hand. "This is pretty damn exciting. I love your tenacious energy and definitely welcome another perspective on cases."

"I love working with you too. And we could always rename the firm if you want to use the **π's for Hire** brand."

"Yeah, let's hold off on that." He gave her a wink as she laughed.

"I'll win you over, boss. Just you wait."

When she returned home, Cyrus was sitting on the couch filling out various papers. Sitting beside him, she looked them over.

"Applications," he said, kissing her shoulder before resuming scribbling the info.

"The security jobs?"

"Yep," he said, nodding. "Three of the different places don't require anything but the GEDs we forged. Hopefully, one of them will hire me."

"Well," she said, settling into the couch and lacing her fingers behind her head, "I got a job today too." His eyes lit up as she told him of her plans with Zander, and he seemed genuinely happy for her.

"You're amazing," he said, squeezing her hand. "I think you'll flourish there."

Her teeth toyed with her lip. "If we both get jobs, we can find a nicer place in D.C."

"Claire," he said, shaking his head.

"I know." She rolled her eyes. "We're taking it day by day."

He chuckled. "One day at time, Finch. Let me secure a job, and then we'll discuss our future. I'm so torn that you're determined to choose me over so many other opportunities you haven't even considered."

"Posh," she said, waving her hand. "I've already chosen you, chief. It's kind of annoying you're fighting it so hard. I hope you decide I'm worth it and choose me back." Standing, she kissed his forehead. "I'm making a sandwich. Want one?"

"Sure."

As she slathered the mustard atop the bread, she smiled, still confident she could win him over if she forged ahead.

"We're going to use the video camera to surveille Sebastian on Thursday right?" she called from the kitchenette.

"Yep, that's when the next meeting of the Knights is in the banquet hall. We'll trail him afterward. If we can get the bastard doing something nefarious on video, we'll at least have some leverage."

Excited to put her newfound sleuthing skills to work, she looked forward to the end of the week.

Chapter 24

Vivian rubbed her eyes, so thankful the long day was almost over. It was Wednesday, which meant she was that much closer to her usual day off on Sunday. Although she was always available to her patients through her pager, she looked forward to the days she got to spend with Marie outside of the clinic.

Carolyn peeked her head around the door and pointed to the chart atop the desk. "That's your last patient," she said, smiling. "I'm heading out for my date. Marie's upstairs cooking a pot roast that smells delicious. You did a good job popping out a kid who loves to cook, Doc."

Chuckling, Vivian nodded. "I did. Last week, she made glazed salmon. I mean, what nine-year-old makes glazed salmon?"

"Only Marie." Carolyn winked. "Do you want me to wait until you see the last patient to leave? I don't mind."

"No," she said, waving her off. "Have fun with Dave. He sounds nice."

"*Dale*," Carolyn corrected. "And he's already been divorced twice, which doesn't give me a lot of hope. But he's sweet and doesn't *seem* like a serial killer..." She rubbed her chin and squinted at the ceiling.

"Be open. You might end up being the third Mrs. Dale," Vivian teased.

"That's definitely some 'do as I say, not as I do' advice, Vivian. When are you going to let Zander take you on a proper date? It's obvious he's dying to ask you out."

Vivian hadn't told Carolyn everything about the man who showed up each night once the sun went down and kept watch on her home. But he'd also stopped by a few times during the day to update her as they uncovered more information, and Carolyn was observant. Vivian rarely showed interest in men, but it was impossible to hide her reaction to Zander. She found him ruggedly handsome and a bit disheveled, which appealed to her somehow. After dating Edward and Jonathan, both of whom were perfectly coiffed at all times, she appreciated Zander's offbeat charm.

"Well, he hasn't asked yet. Probably because I told him I don't date smokers. Think he'll quit for me?"

"Don't know, but if your eyes sparkled like that when you told him, I'd wager he's ready to toss them all and never buy a pack again."

Laughing, Vivian shooed her away. "Go on with your romantic notions. Turn them on Dale. I gave up on that crap a long time ago. Have fun, Carolyn."

"Thanks. I'll send Fred back on my way out."

Vivian picked up the chart, thumbing through it as she digested the new patient's information. He seemed to have some sort of injury to his groin region, which made her ponder if there was an unusual or outlandish story associated with it. Noting his name, her eyebrows drew together. Fred Savage, like the actor. Huffing a laugh, she shook her head. Strange coincidence.

The man knocked on her door, and Vivian stood, gesturing to the chair in front of her desk. "Have a seat, Mr. Savage. You're my last patient today, so we've got plenty of time."

He trailed to the chair with a slight hobble, causing sympathy to well inside.

"Looks like you got injured in a pretty sensitive area. I'm happy to help if I can."

The man adjusted his wire-rimmed glasses before lowering his hands to rest on his thighs. "That's very kind," he said in a low tone. "You know, I missed meeting you in person at the fundraiser, which I now realize was very fortuitous."

"Oh, were you at D.C. Cares? There were so many people there, I barely remember half of them. I wish my memory was better. It's always been pretty terrible."

"Memories are often embellished by our minds," he said, eyes narrowing as he slightly glared. Vivian's heartbeat quickened as warning bells went off in her head. Something about his melancholy tone and soft words sent a shaft of fear down her spine. "I have so many memories of promises I made to powerful men, but now, they all seem to run together. Victor assured me I would be helping the cause, but the men in this era are all consumed by fear. A few pictures of their whores, and they rescind their help and retreat to their fancy homes. What a bunch of pussies. No wonder the Knights eventually disbanded and formed the New Establishment."

Vivian looked out the window, noting the setting sun, thankful Zander would most likely be pulling up soon. Sending a silent prayer to the universe that he would come inside the clinic to check on her, she licked her parched lips, struggling to remain calm.

"Mr. Savage," she said, staring directly into his eyes to showcase her strength. "I realize you're not here for a medical appointment. As you must know, the police chief of the local precinct patrols this area often. I would suggest—"

"The police have no power here," he interrupted, slicing his hand through the air. "No one has true power here. This timeline is a vapid waste of space. But I made a commitment to Victor, and I will see it through."

"What commitment?"

He smirked. "You're an intelligent woman, Vivian. You know I've come here to determine if Marie is Edward's daughter. But the thing is, we both already know the answer. You wouldn't be so careful to remove all traces of her DNA if she wasn't. Why do you hide the truth?"

"Marie is Jonathan Reeves's daughter. She is a child and has nothing to do with my testimony against Dr. Petrov. It's me you want. I have my principles, but my daughter will always be most important. If you commit to leaving us alone, I will agree not to testify against Petrov."

A dark eyebrow arched over his glasses. "You're an excellent liar. Perhaps the Knights should've recruited you instead of Edward. Your deposition against Petrov is already on record, and you're too much of a martyr not to testify in court. Regardless, it's time. Victor assigned me with two tasks: discerning if Marie is Edward's and killing her if she is. Otherwise, the Knights will withdraw their support, and Edward will never make it to the bunker. The New Establishment can only rise if he detonates the nukes. Everything must go according to plan."

"As long as Claire doesn't prevent you from hurting her?" Vivian said, clutching the desk. "Zander told me everything. As unbelievable as it is, he seems to think that Claire will save Marie."

"Unbelievable indeed." He tilted his head. "Which is why I decided to confront you here—when you're alone, and the clinic is quiet, while Marie cooks dinner upstairs. Pot roast, is it? My, how I love a good pot roast."

She began to quake with fear, clenching her teeth together to keep them from rattling. "I won't let you hurt my daughter."

"My dear," he said, pulling the gun from his belt. "She was dead the day Edward knocked you up. I'm sorry. Sometimes, good people must die for the cause." Sliding his finger over the trigger, he aimed it directly between her eyes.

Sliding her hand over the metal letter opener that sat atop her desk, she surreptitiously clutched it in her trembling hand. It wasn't much of a defense against a handgun, but she'd wield it like a damn gladiator in order to save her baby. Allowing the adrenaline to surge into her veins, she prepared to attack.

* * * *

Claire returned home from Zander's office to find a note stuffed under her door. Picking it up, she chuckled as she read the scrawl.

Hi Spy Lady,
Found your address in Cyrus's chart. See? Other people can be spies too. I'm not supposed to write down things from Mom's patients' charts, but I'm nine, so I don't think Lawrence will arrest me. Anyway, I'm making pot roast tonight and thought you and Cyrus might want some. I like him a lot, and you're okay too. There will be a lot of leftovers, and Mom's last patient is at seven. Come over anytime after that if you want.
Your Friend, Marie

The note was absolutely adorable, the signature line causing tears to blur in Claire's eyes. They were friends—in this timeline and the last—and she'd always been such a constant in Claire's life. Deciding she would go to dinner, she set about unloading the groceries she'd picked up on the way home before heading over.

Cyrus was at an interview with a night manager at a local security company, and she wasn't sure when he would be home. They'd finally gotten two phones, so she flipped hers open and tapped the keys to send him a text to meet her at Vivian's clinic. Thankfully, phones in the future would have keyboards instead of her current device's functionality—one tap for "A," two taps for "B," three for "C," and so on. Smiling, she realized how excited she was to navigate the next few decades, hopefully with Cyrus by her side as they cultivated their family. They would get married and experience the explosion of iPads and iPods, tablets and apps—all the fun things Claire understood cerebrally but had never employed in real-life situations. The possibilities were exhilarating to a science geek like her.

140

Once the house was tidy and the groceries put away, she began the walk to Vivian's house, her mouth watering in anticipation of Marie's succulent dinner.

* * * *

Zander pulled up outside of Vivian's clinic, noticing Carolyn exit the front door. She descended the front porch stairs and beelined to his car. Rolling down his window, he smiled as she approached.

"How's the gum treating you?"

"It's terrible," he said, popping another square of the nicotine gum. "But I haven't smoked in a week."

"That's awesome," she said, beaming. "Keep it up, and she'll definitely go out with you."

"I was waiting to ask her until I'd quit for a few weeks."

"Eh, I say go for it. I'm pretty sure she digs you."

"Yeah?" he asked, hope surging in his chest.

"Yep," she said, nodding. "She's tough, but we all have needs, right? Speaking of, I've gotta get going. Have a date tonight."

"Good luck."

"Thanks. We'll see. Vivian's last patient is with her now. Have a good night, Zander. Thanks for keeping an eye on her." With a good-natured salute, she ambled off to catch the bus.

Zander settled in, noticing the black sedan parked on a different corner today. Realizing something was off, his eyes narrowed. Michael was sitting in the passenger side as opposed to behind the wheel. Strange. Did that mean someone else had driven the car to surveil Vivian? If so, where were they?

Blood pounded through his veins, icy and thick, as he observed the house. Carolyn said Vivian was with her last patient...which meant she and Marie were alone in the house with someone.

Deciding he'd risk disturbing her with a patient in order to ensure her safety, he exited the car and drew his gun from the holster. Approaching the front door, he saw Michael exit his vehicle and advance. Turning, he aimed the gun.

"This isn't your fight, Michael," he said, realizing the man was still quite young and his hand trembled slightly as he aimed his firearm. "I know you wanted to be initiated into the Knights. I understand the desire to belong, but they have no use for you. You're just a hired hand to them. Go home to Kaylee and Desiree. Your wife and daughter need you alive."

The man's eyes grew wide. "How do you know—?"

"I'm a P.I.," Zander said. "And you're a young man with a beautiful family. I know you understand deep within that the rich assholes in the Knights will never see you as one of their own. Choose your family. Choose to be better."

"She's pregnant again," he said, shaking his head as he lowered the gun. "I have no idea how we're going to afford two babies."

"It won't be easy, but do you really want to look Desiree in the eye and tell her you helped harm a little girl? Marie is Vivian's child, just like Kaylee is yours. You're better than that, Michael. You can choose to be better."

A police car began to crest the far-off curve, and Zander lowered his gun. "I'm going inside to help Vivian. It's up to you what path you take." Giving him a nod, he left the man on the sidewalk as he rushed toward the house. Pushing open the front door, he saw the empty waiting room and began to make his way down the hallway. Clutching his gun, he pushed open Vivian's office door—and found it empty.

The smell of something cooking upstairs invaded his nostrils, and he began inching toward the stairs. Suddenly, a gun cocked by his ear.

"I'm sorry," Michael whispered. "I'm too deep in this now."

Zander froze, searching for an out. He didn't think the man would actually kill him—he seemed torn and uncertain—but Sebastian certainly would if he came downstairs and found them.

As if on cue, Sebastian's sinister voice spoke from the crest of the stairs. "Well done, Michael. Shoot him. He's a pointless distraction. I have Marie and Vivian sequestered upstairs."

"I don't want you to hurt Marie," Michael said, sweat profusely dripping down his forehead. "I don't want to hurt a little girl. I just want to keep working with the Knights so I can feed my family."

An annoyed sigh left Sebastian's lips as he began to trail down the steps, one by one. "Family. What a ridiculous word. Don't you understand that your family means nothing?" Staring down at them from his perch a few steps above, he aimed his gun at Zander. "Shoot him, Michael, or I will."

Michael struggled with the decision, ultimately sealing his own fate. With a deft stroke of his arm, Sebastian refocused the gun between Michael's eyes and fired. The man crumpled to the floor, lifeless.

"Fuck!" Zander said as he stared as the body. "He had a kid, Sebastian."

"Like I said,"—he shrugged as he descended the last few stairs—"insignificant. I just don't care. My mission got muddled, especially when that bitch maimed me, but we're back on track now." Crooking his fingers, he said, "Give me the gun. Come on. You and your girlfriend can watch while I kill Edward's daughter."

"You don't have to do this—"

"Give me the gun!" Sebastian yelled, appearing crazed as spittle flared from his lips. "Now!"

Deciding to go for it, Zander charged, attempting to wrestle the gun from Sebastian. Even if he was shot, he hoped one of the police cars that patrolled the street would hear the gunfire and rush inside. Although they didn't want cops involved, things were now so dire that Zander would welcome their intervention.

He managed to land two punches, one in Sebastian's side and one in his gut, before his gun dislodged from his hand and slid across the floor. Sebastian retained his weapon and held it to Zander's temple, his breath escaping in small pants.

"Bad move, Zander," he said through gritted teeth. "I was going to let you and Vivian live because Victor told me you were irrelevant, but killing you will be so much more gratifying."

Zander struggled to breathe, wondering if he could still reason with the man, who seemed severely unhinged. Licking his lips and summoning his inner fortitude, he vowed to try.

Before he could speak, a loud blast exploded next to his ear. As if in slow motion, Zander turned, seeing Sebastian's shocked expression before the man clutched his throat and fell to the ground. Lifting his gaze, he saw Claire holding a gun in both hands, the trail of smoke still swirling from the barrel. She gasped air into her lungs, back and forth, as she stared wide-eyed at Sebastian struggling on the floor.

"The gun was just laying there," she explained, staring at the blood pooling on the floor, "and I saw you struggling...and I just picked it up and shot him. Oh, my god." Dropping the firearm, she collapsed, holding her hands to her mouth. "Oh, my god, oh, my god..." Arms wrapped around her upturned knees, she rocked back and forth on the hardwood floor.

"It's okay," Zander said, inching toward her, arm outstretched. "He's bleeding out, Claire. I need to give him a clean shot so he doesn't suffer. Do you understand?"

She nodded furiously, eyes still glued to Sebastian's body as it convulsed on the floor.

"Okay," he said, bending down and picking up Sebastian's gun. "Close your eyes."

She just stared ahead, rocking back and forth.

"Claire, close your eyes."

When she complied, he aimed the gun at Sebastian's temple and delivered one clean shot. Claire's entire body jerked as Sebastian expelled his final breath, his frame falling still in the pooled blood.

"You're okay," Zander soothed, sitting beside her and drawing her into his embrace. "You're okay. You saved them, Claire, just like Sebastian predicted. Holy shit, you saved Marie."

"I saved her." Tears doused his neck as she violently sobbed against him. "I didn't mean to kill him."

"I know," he said into her hair, wishing he could think of something that would console her. "It's okay."

"Zander!" a voice called from upstairs. "Are you okay? Marie and I are tied up in the kitchen."

"We're okay!" he yelled. "Are you guys all right?"

"We're fine!"

Something seemed to explode behind him, and he turned to see Cyrus burst through the front door. "I heard gunshots," he said, taking in the scene. "What the fuck happened?"

"Cyrus!" Claire called, shaking her head as tears streamed down her face. "I didn't mean to. I swear."

"Sweetheart," he whispered, dropping to his knees and taking her into his arms. His hands roved over her face, her arms, her stomach, looking for injuries.

"She's not hurt," Zander said, standing and glancing up the stairs. "But Marie and Vivian are restrained upstairs."

"Go," Cyrus said, holding Claire against his body. "I'll take care of her. I'm sure the police heard the gunshots and will be here any minute."

Zander reached into his pocket and threw him the keys. "The car's across the street. Get her out of here. We don't want them tracing you when you're trying to build an unblemished backstory. I'll say I shot Sebastian and Michael."

"Thank you," Cyrus said, scooping Claire into his arms and heading out the door. "We'll call later."

Zander crooked his head and all but ran up the stairs, finding Vivian and Marie tied to the kitchen chairs. He untied Vivian first, then Marie, and the girl threw herself into his arms.

"I was really scared," she whispered into his ear.

"I know," he said, squeezing her as he stroked her soft hair. "It's okay. I won't ever let anyone hurt you."

"Or Mom."

"Or your mom," he said, unable to control his smile. "I kind of like her. A lot."

"She likes you too," she said, rubbing her wet nose on his shirt. Hell, he didn't even care. The little imp had grown on him over these past few weeks, and she was an extension of Vivian. Since he was completely besotted by the woman, it made sense he would cherish her daughter too.

"Yeah?" he asked. Swiping his thumbs across her wet cheeks, he asked softly, "Do you think she might go out on a date with me sometime?"

"I don't know." Marie shrugged. "But if she does, make sure you don't lick her."

A laugh escaped his throat. "Lick her?"

"Yeah. Adam Goldstein tried to lick me when we kissed under the monkey bars. It was so gross."

"Okay," he said, squeezing his lips together. The kid was hilarious. "Good advice. Thanks."

"Come here, young lady," Vivian said, crouching beside them and pulling her into a tight embrace. "I'm so glad you're okay." She trailed kisses over her hair, a smile across her gorgeous face as she marveled at her daughter's sage advice. "And we're going to have a nice long talk about why Adam Goldstein is kissing you at school."

"Whatever, Mom," she said, swiping her arm over her nose. "He's not even in the picture anymore."

Zander leaned his elbow over his bent knee and covered his mouth, gazing at Vivian. She shook her head and pointed at her daughter, her expression of mock disbelief at the extremely mature words.

She clutched his hand and drew him close, sliding her arm around his shoulders. "Thank you," she whispered.

"You're welcome," he said, cupping her cheek. The three of them sat huddled on the floor as the sirens wailed in the distance. "Did you hear Claire and Cyrus downstairs?"

Vivian nodded. "They're gone?"

"Yes. I'm going to say I shot Sebastian and Michael. My gun is registered, and it was in self-defense."

"I invited Claire over for dinner," Marie said, frowning as she looked at the cooled pot roast atop the stove. "Guess she decided to come."

"My sweet girl," Vivian said, kissing her on the cheek before wiping away the gloss left behind. "Don't tell the police they were here, okay? We'll invite her and Cyrus over again another day."

Marie nodded. "I can't give away Claire's identity. Her spy work is really important."

"Is that so?" Vivian asked.

"Yeah. Something about knights and evil people and the future. I haven't figured out who they are yet, but I hear everything. They talked about it all night at the fundraiser. Not too smart for spies. They should probably whisper."

"We'll make sure to tell them that when they come for dinner," she said as they stood. "If the policemen ask you any questions, just tell them to talk to me, okay?"

"Got it, Mom," she said, rolling her eyes.

A voice called Vivian's name from downstairs. "That's Lawrence," she said.

Zander extended his hands, one to each of the women who'd stolen his heart. "Up here," he called, not wanting to lead Marie downstairs where the bodies were. "We're in the kitchen, officers."

Squeezing their hands, he silently communicated his vow to protect them. Straightening his shoulders, he awaited the police, ready to put this case far behind him.

Chapter 25

Cyrus carried Claire inside, locking the door behind them and sitting on the couch. Situating her across his lap, he soothed her, letting her cry into the juncture where his neck met his shoulder. Eventually, the sobs turned to hiccups, and he stroked her hair, thankful she was regaining some composure.

Lifting her head, she stared at him, those wet eyes achingly beautiful. "How do I reconcile this?"

"It's tough," he said, stroking the hair at her temple. "Believe me."

Inhaling a ragged breath, she slid her hand over his jaw. "We'll both always have blood on our hands. Sebastian's on mine, and Dalton's on yours."

Silent, he contemplated her. In equating their transgressions, it was obvious she longed to have him absolve her—absolve them both—but absolution wasn't his to give. Was it?

"I need time to process this. I'd also like to ensure he has a gravesite since he didn't have any family in this timeline."

"Doc Viv can probably help us arrange that."

"Yes," she whispered.

They embraced for a while, absorbing the events, until she lifted her gaze to his. "I won't let this ruin my life, Cyrus. What happened with Sebastian was awful, but it saved Marie's life. Hell, it probably saved *my* life, and it's a life I'm determined to live to the fullest. I feel *alive* for the first time in so long and really thrive here. *We* thrive here. Together."

"Claire—"

"No, Cyrus. No more fear. Today taught me I can't squander one more moment. I need you to choose me. It's time."

"Time," he murmured, caressing her wet cheek. "I feel like time has been steering me toward you for so long, in ways I never even comprehended."

She gave him a warbled smile. "That's pretty poetic, chief."

Feeling his lips quirk, he pressed them to hers for a poignant kiss. "Can we talk about the future tomorrow? I know we need to make some firm decisions, but I just want to hold you tonight, sweetheart."

Wrapping her arms around his neck, she whispered softly against his lips. "I want that too."

They showered together in the small bathroom before he carried her to bed, marveling at the flush of her skin from the steam. Enveloping her in a spooning embrace, he buried his face in her neck as she shimmied the globes of her magnificent ass against his shaft. Too exhausted to make love, they fell asleep, the tips of her hair tickling his chin as his strong arms protected her from nightmares.

* * * *

Cyrus awoke, lids snapping open as he scanned the darkened room. Years of military training caused his muscles to tense as he sensed a presence. Someone was outside. Glancing down at Claire, she slept, open-mouthed, as she drooled onto the pillow. For some reason, it was hands-down the most enchanting thing he'd ever seen. Inwardly muttering that he'd gone full-on sap, he gently extricated himself from her body and pulled on some shorts, a T-shirt, and athletic slip-ons. Clutching his gun, he left the apartment, locking both deadbolts behind him.

Quietly, he crept down the stairs and outside to the yard. A gentle breeze caressed his skin, causing him to shiver. Behind him, a twig snapped, and he pivoted, aiming the gun.

"Whoa there, Captain Montgomery," Lainey said, holding up her hands. "You wouldn't shoot a friend, would you?"

Disbelief coursed through his frame. "Lainey? How are you here?"

She smiled, her vibrant eyes sparkling in the moonlight. "Um, I built a time machine, in case you forgot."

Lowering the gun, he set it on the soft grass. "Are you here to transport us to 2035?"

Lainey's lips curved as she shook her head. "No way. You were adamant when you came to me that you and Claire were happy here. So you're staying, buddy."

Confusion twirled the gears in his brain as he struggled to comprehend the cryptic conversation. "Am I dreaming?"

"Maybe," she said, shrugging. "I've come to realize this all might be a dream. Hell, maybe every single timeline is, and we're just pawns in someone else's game. Pawns of Paradoxes. I like it. I'd play that any day."

Cyrus stayed silent, blood thrumming throughout his body.

"Have you asked Claire to marry you yet?"

His brows lifted. "No, but I'm close. I've come up with a million reasons why it won't work between us. But tonight, as I was holding her...after everything we've been through together in this timeline..." His gaze fell to the ground as comprehension swamped him. "I don't think I can live without her."

Lainey's teeth all but flashed in the starlight as she smiled. "You love her."

"I love her," he said with a nod.

Sighing, she closed her eyes, lifting her face to the sky. "I fought my feelings for Hunter too until you talked some sense into me."

"I did?"

"Yes. That's why I'm here. You come to visit me in 2035, when you're in your seventies. I'm going to tell you everything so you'll know exactly where to find me on that specific date and what to say to me, okay?"

Rubbing the back of his neck, he said, "Uh, okay."

Her chuckle surrounded them. "I know. It's so freaking strange. But, for better or for worse, we're victims of the events we all created in previous timelines. If we follow the clues our previous selves have left behind, I know we can ultimately prevail."

"What exact point in time did you travel from?" he asked, the curiosity overwhelming.

"August 2035. We're so close to confronting my grandfather. All the pieces are falling into place. You know my cynical scientific heart doesn't believe in fate or destiny or any of that crap,"—she waved a dismissive hand—"but, honestly, this time? I just might. I feel it in my bones, Cyrus. We *have* to win."

"Then we will," he said, giving into the urge to pull her into his arms. Embracing her, he spoke against her hair. "Tell me what I need to do, and I'll update you on everything we've uncovered, starting with the Knights of Washington."

Drawing back, she squeezed his arms. "Well, obviously, you need to marry Claire. You got that part, right?"

"Got it," he said, grinning.

"Okay, then let me tell you the rest." Stepping back, she held up her hand and began ticking off items on her fingers. "First, you need to come find me on May 3, 2035..."

Cyrus listened intently, his fastidious mind relegating everything to memory. Once he returned inside, he would write it down, just in case, but he now understood so many things.

When Lainey had divulged everything and he'd apprised her of all he'd learned, he gave her one last hug and headed back up to the apartment, noticing the bright flash of light from the back yard.

Sliding into bed beside Claire, her pulse hummed against his face as he surrounded her with his body.

"Where did you go?" she mumbled into the pillow.

"Outside. I'll tell you tomorrow."

She wiggled her butt into the juncture of his thighs, and he kissed her neck, wanting so badly to finally tell her he loved her but knowing it wasn't the right time.

"Don't leave me, Cyrus," she whispered in the darkness.

His eyebrows drew together at the statement. "I'll never leave you, sweetheart."

"Promise?"

"Mm-hmm..." he murmured, feeling his eyelids grow heavy.

In seconds, he was lost to dreams, never realizing she was wide-awake as he held her.

Chapter 26

Claire whipped the eggs and milk together in the bowl, the furious motions reflecting the anger that burned in her gut. Glancing at Cyrus as he sat on the couch reading, she scowled. It had been three days—the longest three days of her life—since she awoke to find the bed empty. Trailing to the window, she'd observed Cyrus speaking to Lainey, and her heart had all but fallen through the floor.

Of course, she was elated to see her friend, whom she missed vehemently, and was thrilled she appeared to be healthy and unharmed. But she'd also felt trepidation at Lainey's appearance. She must've come to abscond with them to 2035. Back to the cause...to the fight she firmly believed in, but in which she no longer wanted to be entrenched. Just when Claire had found a timeline in which she was abundantly happy—and had almost convinced Cyrus to love her back—her friend had appeared to whisk them away.

She'd lay back down, giving Cyrus ample opportunity to tell her what the hell was going on, but he hadn't uttered a word about it in days. Not understanding why he still hadn't told her and wondering what he was waiting for, she slammed the bowl on the counter. Cyrus was at her side in two seconds flat, a comforting hand on her shoulder.

"Finch?" he asked, gently turning her to face him. "What's wrong?"

Glowering at him, she punched him in the arm.

"Ouch! What was that for?"

"What's wrong?" she asked, placing her hands on her hips. "You've had three days to tell me about Lainey's visit." She held up three fingers. "Three days, Cyrus! What gives? Why didn't you wake me up so I could talk to her? Are you waiting to break it to me gently that she's taking us to 2035, because I'm pretty pissed you're keeping secrets from me?"

Amusement entered his eyes, and she waggled her finger at him. "You do *not* get to laugh right now."

Chuckling, he tried to slide his arms around her.

"Nope," she said, placing her palms on his pecs. "No hanky-panky until you tell me what the hell is going on."

"Claire—"

"Don't you 'Claire' me, mister. You know, I'm actually pretty damn smart, and if you think for one moment—"

His lips overtook hers, inhaling the words as he dragged her into his body. Lost to the blazing desire she always felt for him, her body relaxed in his embrace, thus proving she never stood a chance at being mad at him. Arousal hummed in her veins as his lips and tongue worked their glorious magic until he broke the kiss and smiled into her eyes.

"Will you let me talk for a damn minute, Finch?"

Man, her lips were on fire. The man could kiss. Blinking to clear her frazzled brain, she nodded.

"Fine, but only because I've lost all control of my body."

His lips curved as he rested his forehead on hers. "Claire," he whispered, threading his fingers through her hair, cupping her head, as his other hand splayed over her lower back. When he drew back, she noticed how clear his eyes were as he spoke. "I love you. Haven't you figured that out by now?"

Her knees buckled—legitimately losing all semblance of substance—but her strong soldier caught her, as he always did. Biting her lip, she caressed his face.

"You do?"

His eyes darted to the ceiling as if he couldn't believe she was even asking. Locking back onto her, he said, "Yes, sweetheart."

"Then why didn't you tell me about Lainey? Why didn't you come get me so I could see her? Are we going to 2035? I'm so freaking confused."

"I didn't wake you because she told me not to."

"Why? I would've loved to hug her and ask her what the hell is going on. I feel like I'm *really* out of the loop here."

"I think she wanted you to be surprised. I'm pretty sure our resident cynical scientist is actually a romantic at heart. Seems like Rhodes might've softened her a bit. Who would've guessed?"

Claire's eyebrows drew together. "Surprised by what?"

Straightening, he gently disengaged from her embrace. "Stay here, okay? One sec."

After ambling to the bedroom, he returned with a small bag. When he pulled out a box, she lifted her hand to her mouth, hope surging deep within.

"I bought this yesterday," he said, lowering to one knee as he opened the box. A silver ring with a tiny diamond was nestled inside. "I didn't want to tell you until I could propose. I don't know." He shrugged. "It seemed more romantic or something."

She began to sob, and he grabbed her wrist, tugging on it as he laughed. "Whoa, hold on. No crying yet. I need to ask you to marry me first. This ring isn't much, but hopefully, once I get settled in the security job, I can buy you a bigger one."

"It's beautiful," she said, tears streaming down her cheeks.

"I'm not going anywhere with Lainey, and neither are you. You love it here—which you've been pretty damn clear about—and I love being anywhere you are. So we're staying. I choose you, Claire. Wherever and whenever in time you are, I'll always choose you. Will you marry me?"

Unable to answer, she nodded furiously and lowered to her knees, wrapping her arms around his neck and placing fervent kisses all over his face. Eventually, she relented so he could slip the ring on her finger. Gazing at it through her tears, she beamed at him.

"You chose me."

"Always," he said, kissing her softly.

Throwing her head back and giving a joyous whoop, she latched onto his hand and dragged him to the bedroom. "Okay, this was epic. You get whatever you want, chief. Bondage, submission, triple blow job—you name it. Let's get naked."

Burying his face in his hands, his body shook with laughter. "You're too much, Finch," he said, elation encompassing his handsome features. "What the hell is a triple blow job?"

"It sounded sexy," she said, tossing her shirt on the floor and shucking the rest of her clothes behind it. "Let's find out."

Naked, she balanced on her hands and knees on the bed. "Come here, soldier," she said, crooking her finger. He walked toward her, and she all but tore his clothes off before reaching for his shaft.

"Sweetheart..." he breathed, threading his fingers through her hair as she placed kisses along his sensitive, swollen length.

Eyes glued to his, she took him in her mouth, loving the smooth texture of his skin against her tongue and the salty essence that was Cyrus. Strong fingers tightened in her hair as he began to pump his hips into her, driving her insane with lust as he lost the tendrils of control.

"God, Claire," he whispered, his voice raspy as he undulated into her. "Look how sexy you are."

She groaned around the straining flesh, feeling her inner walls quiver and flush with wetness. Moaning, he popped from her lips and flipped her on her stomach, crawling over her and cementing his lips to the shell of her ear.

"Do you want me to get a condom?"

"No," she said, wiggling into him.

His broad hands spread her ass wide as he searched for her drenched opening. Pressing his face against hers, he slid into her from behind.

"This is definitely going to make babies," he said, pumping into her. "Are you ready for that, sweetheart?"

"God, yes," she cried, head thrown back as his fingers found the sensitive nub between her slick folds. Circling it in a maddening rhythm as he jutted into her from behind, she damn near experienced heaven. "I love you," she moaned, opening her body to him, giving him every last piece of her heart.

"I love you so much, sweetheart." The low-toned words caused every cell in her body to quiver as he brought her to her peak. Finally, when she could take no more, she shattered in his arms, her body limp as he found his own release. Mired in bliss, she reveled in each and every twitch of his skin against hers as he emptied inside her. Snuggling into him, their breaths mingled as they struggled to regain composure.

"Damn, Finch," he said, nipping her earlobe as she damn near giggled. "That was one impressive blow job."

Chuckling, she nodded. "Next time, I'll get on my knees, and you can tie my hands behind my back."

He shuddered and bit her neck. "I'm pretty sure my brain just exploded from that mental image."

Laughing, she relaxed against him. They lounged, lazy and sated, as she drew random patterns across his arm with her fingertips.

"My god, we get to build our lives from scratch, Cyrus. Do you realize how incredibly lucky we are?"

"So lucky. Now that Sebastian's gone, the threat from the Knights has lessened, but I'll remain on high alert. If we're diligent and careful, I think we can build a life separate from Randolph and anything having to do with him."

"A life where we don't have to save the world. How strange."

"There are still pieces that need to fall in place. I'll tell you everything I discussed with Lainey once I recover."

"I can't wait to hear," she said, feeling her eyes droop. "I miss Lainey...but not enough to leave this timeline and rejoin the fight. Does that make me selfish?"

"No. It makes you human. Didn't you say that to me once before?"

"I did," she said, tilting her head.

"Then let's remember that as we build our life together. It won't be perfect, but it will be ours. Something new and exciting."

"Can't wait. You're going to be such an amazing father, Cyrus."

"With you by my side, I think I can do it, Finch." His breath grew heavy against her neck, and she let herself fade, feeling so safe and protected in his arms. Thrilled to experience the future with the man who'd held her heart for so long, she sent a silent prayer of thanks to Eli for raiding the hub and inadvertently sending them to 2002. Would he and the others prevail in 2035? She didn't know. But no one was stronger and more determined than her team of amazing friends, and she couldn't wait to reconnect with them in the future, once they'd hopefully prevented the past.

Chapter 27

October 2034

Dr. Vivian Elders observed the professor as he finished up his class. He was an excellent teacher, and his love of physics was evident. Reminding his students there would be a test on Friday, he dismissed them and began stacking papers on his desk.

Vivian waited until everyone had dispersed before approaching.

"Hello," he said, smiling politely. "You're not one of my usual students, but I love having walk-ins. Did you enjoy the class?"

"I did," she said truthfully. "Your discussion on Dr. Mallett's theories was fascinating."

"Thank you," he said, excitement in his eyes. "He was ahead of his time, that's for sure. Are you also a physicist?"

"I'm a doctor but not a PhD. MD over here. Just good ol'-fashioned general medicine."

"We need general practitioners now more than ever. It's a pleasure to meet you..."

"Vivian," she said, extending her elbow, which had become the norm ever since the coronavirus pandemic in 2020.

"Well, hello, Vivian. Lewis Randolph. Nice to meet you." He bumped her elbow with his. "I appreciate you observing the class. Most of my students usually browse dating or internet apps while they pretend to listen to me."

"They seemed enthralled. You don't give yourself enough credit."

"From your lips to Carl Sagan's ears," he said with a sparkle in his eye. When her eyebrows drew together, he said, "It's a joke I have with my partner, Nelson. Since we're atheists, we send our prayers to scientists. Sagan, deGrasse Tyson, Einstein. You get the drift."

"Got it," she said with a nod. "So Dr. Mallett's theories. Do you think you could ever get them to work?"

"In reality?" he asked, rubbing his chin. "Possibly, but there would have to be a cataclysmic event that would push me toward it. It would require years of intense focus and dedication, and I'd have to stop teaching the great future minds of America." He gestured to the empty seats, amusement in his tone. "Why do you ask?"

Her eyes darted between his, and she noticed the flecks of yellow within the hazel irises. "I've experienced a lot of things in my life. Running my clinic was a grind, and I saw the best and worst of humanity. I'm retired now, which my husband is thankful for because he actually gets to see me."

"Don't tell my wife," Lewis joked. "She'll be jealous. Says I spend too much time in the lab with Nelson."

"I get it, believe me. People like us are dedicated to the cause."

"The cause... I like that," he said thoughtfully.

"Yes, to make the world a better place. Usually, we make small strides for good, but the bad guys always seem to win. I've never figured out why."

"Seeming to win and *actually* winning are two different things, Vivian. My optimistic heart truly believes that."

"Then I've done the right thing by approaching you," she said, a warm cloud of relief blanketing her body.

"I'm not sure I follow."

"I have a daughter, Marie. She's recently divorced and has a son, George. He's pretty much the light of both our lives."

"That's lovely," he said. "My wife and I hope to have kids soon, but I need to do more of that whole 'be at home' thing we discussed." He gave a mock grimace.

Chuckling, she nodded. "I get it. I hope it happens for you soon. Once you have a child, you'll realize you'd do anything to protect them. Even if they're over forty, as Marie is now."

Lewis remained polite, although she could tell he was beginning to think she was slightly unhinged. "Years ago, I met a lovely couple, although they weren't a couple at the time. Claire and Cyrus. Do those names mean anything to you?"

"Can't say they do. Were they possibly students of mine?"

"Perhaps," she said, thinking of Claire. "I'm not entirely sure. Regardless, they were close with my husband and told him things he eventually passed on to me. Things I didn't believe until recently, when I began to see the trajectory the world has taken, especially with your father's followers."

Lewis sighed before his lips drew into a thin line. "My father and I are as different as two opposite poles of a magnet. I'm not in politics and try to stay as far away as possible."

"But you disagree with his views."

"Yes," Lewis said, his shoulders hunched. "Honestly, I sometimes doubt whether he believes half of them himself. But he's beholden to his base, and the movement has grown beyond him. He's just a figurehead at this point. That's what I tell myself, anyway, so I can sleep at night."

Vivian digested the information, hoping against all odds that Edward could find the soul he'd lost so long ago. That the man she'd once loved still had a sliver of goodness.

"It's an interesting perspective," she said, reaching into her pocket and pulling out an envelope. "I hope you're right." Extending the envelope, she urged him to take it. "I'll ask you to read that once I'm gone and when you have time to digest it. I'm not a spring chicken anymore and have been diagnosed with cancer. My husband has COPD from smoking for many years before I met him and isn't in the best of health. Being a physician, I know we're both bound to go sooner rather than later."

"I'm very sorry to hear that, Vivian," he said, clutching the letter.

"Thank you. We all have our time, and I've had a good life. I wouldn't change a damn thing." Comforted by his grin, she continued. "I have absolutely no right to ask this of you, but I would like to ensure Marie and George have someone to watch out for them if I'm gone."

Shock laced his features. "I, um...I'm not sure if I'm the right person to ask—"

"You're the only person to ask. You and Marie are tied together through actions that occurred many decades ago. It was selfish not to tell either of you, and now I'm about to die, and I need to make things right."

"Sorry, but I have no idea what you're speaking of, Vivian. If you're unwell, we should get you to the hospital."

"I know," she said, rubbing her forehead with her fingers. "I sound insane. Half the time, I think I am. The letter will explain your connection to her. You can choose whether to tell her or not. I haven't informed her and recently realized I can't bring myself to do it. For some reason, it's so much easier to tell your secrets to a stranger. Why is that?"

He contemplated her, appearing compassionate and perplexed. "I don't know."

"Thank you, Lewis. For listening to an old woman rant. I wish you success, although I think it will come at a hefty price. Most great successes do. Regardless, I have every faith that you or someone you pass the mantle to will prevail. When that day comes, I'll rejoice, wherever I am in this infinite universe. Take care of yourself. I'll be cheering you on and sending every ounce of positive energy your way."

Unable to suppress her rapidly forming tears, she pivoted and exited the classroom, thankful he'd taken the letter. Inside was the confirmation Marie was his half-sister and George his half-nephew. She had no idea if he would accept the information or tell Marie but somehow understood that he would reach out to her, if only out of curiosity at first. But Marie would charm him, as she did everyone, and if there was an imminent disaster, she truly believed Lewis would welcome her into his fold and protect her.

"How'd it go?" Zander asked when she slid into the passenger seat.

"Good," she said, exhaling in relief. "I think he'll make contact, and, hopefully, they'll form a bond. If there truly is an apocalypse, I think he'll feel a compulsion to safeguard her. Who knows? They could become fast friends."

"That they could." Gripping her hand, he squeezed, both of them wrinkled as they clutched together. "Ready?"

"Ready."

She held his hand the entire way, realizing how much she would miss small displays of affection and the warmth of his skin against hers.

"After all this time, I still clutch onto everything Claire and Cyrus have told us about who Marie becomes in the future."

"That she lived to be a very old woman and was feisty as hell?"

Nodding, Vivian felt the tear trail down her cheek. It was all she'd ever wanted for her daughter—to live a long, full life, complete and joyful. Thankful for the confirmation, she held tight to her husband, overcome with gratitude that she'd also experienced those things.

"I love you," she whispered to Zander.

"Love you too, sweetheart."

Wiping the wetness from her cheek, she relaxed into the seat and proceeded to tell her husband no less than eight times he was driving too slow and missed several turns. When they arrived home, he punished her with a multitude of sloppy kisses across her face and neck, which weren't punishment at all. They were sweet, playful expressions of love, and she relished each and every one.

Chapter 28

Late March 2035

Victor Hernandez approached the unmarked grave, unmoved by the darkened hollows of the cemetery. Perhaps the man he was meeting thought the tales of ghosts and goblins who haunted the site would give him pause, but Victor understood that evil existed in potent form without needing to hide in shadows. For that fact, he was grateful, because that glaring evil would help him implement his plans.

The man wore a long trench coat and hat, covering his face. Victor approached and slid his hands into his pockets, waiting. Observing the grave, he asked, "Whose is it?"

The man's lashes moved in the moonlight as he blinked, although Victor still couldn't discern his features. "His name was Sebastian. He was sent on an important mission that he never truly understood. He thought his goal was to keep a woman from saving a young girl, but, in truth, we needed that woman to kill Sebastian. His actions affirm her husband's resolve to protect her and eventually marry her, and their daughter becomes vital to Randolph's 2032 election."

"Who is she? I know all of the women who work in Randolph's administration."

The man waved a dismissive hand. "It doesn't matter. She's done her part, helping Randolph get crucial votes from demographics he never would've won on his own. Sebastian's mission was successful, although he may not have liked the outcome." His gaze was fixed on the weathered headstone. "Vivian ensured he received a gravesite since he subsisted only briefly in their timeline. She truly was altruistic. If more people like her existed on the planet, perhaps we wouldn't have to purge it."

Victor's eyebrows drew together as he spoke of her in the past tense. "She's dead?"

The man nodded. "Cancer took her in January."

"Were you close?"

Scoffing, he shook his head. "Not even a little bit. She hated everything we stand for."

Looking the man up and down, he asked, "So you're a member of the New Establishment too?"

Turning, he pushed the hat, revealing his face, and Victor gasped. "Yes. As you can see, I'm the most important member."

"How?" Victor whispered.

"I need you to listen to me very carefully, Victor. You're going to find Puss in Boots tomorrow. I remember when I first found him, all those decades ago. It took me years to put it together. So much time wasted before I began to travel back and attempt to contact you. Finally, I believe this cycle will be successful."

"But you're..." He lifted his hands, slightly reaching toward the other man. "You're..."

"Yes, I'm you, although many years older. I'm here to help ensure President Randolph's success. It is imperative he makes it to the bunker on the fourth of September and detonates the nukes. Every piece must fall into place. Do you understand?"

Victor struggled to process the strange words from someone who was undoubtedly...*him*. Still, his desire to succeed was strong, and it slowly began to override his doubt.

"What do I need to do?"

The man's lips twitched. "Good. You've been somewhat disbelieving when approached in previous timelines. Perhaps this time will truly be different."

"I see the change in Randolph. Every day we grow closer to implementing the plan, his resolve seems to waver."

"It will continue to do so. You must listen to me very carefully. This time, we cannot fail. And if things go exactly as planned, we have decided to kill Lewis after the apocalypse in this cycle."

"The president's son? He's a scientist who isn't involved with Randolph's political career."

"He trains his daughter, and she eventually constructs the functioning time machine. We need her to succeed in that—and we have let her succeed in every timeline. But this time, if things go exactly as planned, we will ensure she's never born. This time, we could end the cycle once and for all."

"And the New Establishment will rise to prominence."

"Yes. It will take many decades, and there will be much resistance, but it will eventually prevail. Lainey must succeed one last time. We must let her team converge upon the bunker. There are things that must happen at that one moment in time. It's a precarious balance, fighting her cause while still striving for her success."

"Tell me everything," Victor said, spine straight as every last vestige of doubt dissolved. "I won't fail this time."

"Good," the older man said. "There is much to learn. Most importantly, make sure you don't touch me. Lainey and Lewis are convinced that different versions of one's self can't make physical contact. Although I have no idea if it's true, let's err on the side of caution."

Victor nodded, trailing beside the man as he began a slow pace through the cemetery.

"First, you'll encounter Lainey tomorrow in the alley where Puss in Boots appears. The cat is the very first live subject to travel through time, and you'll discover him there. There is much you'll say to her and much she doesn't know. You'll only have a few minutes before Jamal appears..."

As he listened to the man for hours, Victor tried his best to digest the information. Unless every detail was perfect, they would repeat the cycle again. Determined they would prevail *this* time, Victor reveled in the supremacy he was so close to obtaining...

* * * *

Drunk with power, Victor never realized a young woman was watching them from the trees, secretly intent on helping the cause, albeit the opposing side. Eventually, the woman returned to her car and checked her messages, replying to one her mom had sent hours ago.

iMessage: I'm okay. Sorry I missed your text. Late night at the office.

Mom: Oh, posh. You'd better not be pulling all-nighters again. Love you, sweetie.

iMessage: Love you. See you for dinner tomorrow night. French toast?

Mom: Oh, yes. I'll tell your father. See you then.

Setting the phone down, she drove home, desperate to hug her husband once he returned from his night shift at the hospital. Placing her hand over her still-flat abdomen, she made a promise to the child inside that this would be the last cycle.

That was one thing upon which she and Victor Hernandez were deadlocked in agreement.

Epilogue

October 2009

Claire stared at the magnificence that was her husband. Head resting on her hand atop her elbow, she let her eyes wander over his handsome face as love pervaded every cell in her body. His long, black lashes rested against his cheeks as he breathed deeply.

She should let him sleep. After all, he'd worked the late shift at his security post for the government buildings he guarded. But he was so damn sexy, and she just...god, she needed to touch him.

"Why are you staring at me, Finch?" he mumbled, eyes still closed.

She snickered and rubbed her leg against his. "Because I want to ravish your body."

"Mmm..." Gliding his arm under her side, he lifted her to sprawl atop his still-waking frame. Sliding his lids open, his deep mahogany irises were filled with desire. "Go ahead. Ravish away."

Claire damn near giggled as she kissed a trail down his scruffy jaw, toward his neck and over his bare chest. Still awed by his gorgeous body even after several years of marriage, she glided her palms over his pecs.

"You're so hot, chief."

Full lips curved as he stroked her hair. "I like the orange highlights," he said, twisting a strand of her colored hair around his finger.

"It looks ridiculous," she said, rolling her eyes. "But I'm so damn addicted to the hair products in this timeline. You're sweet to still compliment your wife."

"I wouldn't care if you shaved it all off and dyed your whole head green. You'd still be the most beautiful woman I've ever seen, Claire."

Tears stung her eyes as her heart melted. "I love you," she whispered.

He gazed down at her, stroking her cheek as she nuzzled into his broad hand. Wanting to reward her husband for his extremely caring words, she began to kiss a trail down his abdomen, loving how the muscles trembled beneath her lips.

"Sweetheart—" he whispered.

"Shh," she interrupted, grinning up at him.

Suddenly, they both froze and stared at the door.

"Did you hear that?" she asked softly.

"Yes." She could almost see his ears perk as he squinted at the door.

"Footsteps. I thought we were safe in here. Do you think they're going to attack?"

He nodded. "In about five seconds."

Claire's heart pounded as she waited for the assault.

Suddenly, the door swung open, and two bodies charged into the room. Jumping on the bed, they screamed, "Happy birthday, Mommy!"

Claire laughed with joy, rolling onto her back to hug her babies. They crawled over every inch of the bed, dispersing wet kisses.

"Are you ready for your surprises, Mommy?" Jamal asked, so thoughtful like his father.

"Yes, sweetie," she said, cupping his jaw. "I can't wait to see what you have planned."

"So many surprises, right, guys?" Cyrus asked, drawing them both into his embrace. "All day long, even after bedtime."

"What can you do after bedtime?" Elaine asked, wrinkling her nose.

"Daddy's going to hold Mommy and make her smile. Right, Mommy?"

"Oh, heck yes," Claire said, already anticipating his sweet lovin'. "Mommy can't wait."

Cyrus winked at her as the kids crawled over them, excited about the day's events. They played a while, Cyrus tickling them both until they dissolved in laughter.

"Okay, who wants French toast?" she asked.

"Oh, me, me, me!" they both called, raising their hands.

"Go on in the kitchen and let us get dressed. We'll be right there."

The kids scrambled off the bed and out of the room as Cyrus rolled over her.

"Finch, your kids are way too rambunctious for this old man."

"*Your* kids are riled up because you make my birthday such a big deal. I told you that you didn't have to do that anymore."

"I love celebrating you, honey," he said, giving her a sweet kiss. "And so do they."

"From post-apocalyptic nail polish to two great kids. We've come a long way."

"We have." His thumb caressed her lips.

"Thank you for choosing me," she said, "and this life here. I know you could've made other choices."

"That's not true," he said, shaking his head. "I never had a choice when it came to you. It just took me a while to figure it out. I love you so much, Claire."

"Damn it," she said, swallowing thickly. "Are you really going to make me cry on my birthday?"

Chuckling, he gave her one last kiss before slowly rising. Extending his hand, he said, "Come on, honey. I'm dying for your scrumptious French toast."

Grasping her husband's hand, she let him drag her into the day—one of many birthdays she would share with her beloved family.

Before You Go

Well, Dear Reader, I'm *dying* to know...did you fall in love with Cyrus and Claire as much as I did? I really hope so! Man, they're such awesome characters, and I adored each minute I spent writing their book.

Ready to find out what happened to Alora, Zach, Eli, Elle, and the others stranded in 2075 (and maybe meet Cyrus and Claire's daughter)? Order their book, **A Timeline Restored**—the exciting conclusion to the Prevent the Past trilogy!

* * * *

Please consider leaving a review on Amazon, Goodreads, and/or BookBub. Indie authors survive on reviews and they are so appreciated. Your friendly neighborhood author thanks you from the bottom of her heart!

* * * *

<u>**Books by Rebecca Hefner**</u>

<u>**Prevent the Past Series**</u>
Book 1: A Paradox of Fates
Book 2: A Destiny Reborn
Book 3: A Timeline Restored

<u>**The Etherya's Earth Series (Fantasy/Paranormal Romance)**</u>
Book 1: The End of Hatred
Book 2: The Elusive Sun
Book 3: The Darkness Within
Book 4: The Reluctant Savior
Book 4.5: Immortal Beginnings (in the Untouched Heroes anthology)
Book 5: The Impassioned Choice
Book 5.5: Two Souls United
Book 6: The Cryptic Prophecy
Book 6.5: Garridan's Mate (in the Hearts Unleashed anthology)
Book 7: Coming soon!

<h1 style="text-align:center">Acknowledgments</h1>

Well, here we are again. Now that I'm publishing my seventh book under this name (perhaps another twist indicating I have other nom de plumes?), I'm beginning to find my groove as an author. Don't get me wrong—it's *hard*. There are so many days I question myself and wonder if I'm on the right path. I'm constantly trying to grow and challenge myself, and this book was certainly my biggest challenge to date.

When I began writing the Prevent the Past series, I wanted to ensure it had a cast of diverse characters that represented the world in which we all live. I didn't want to fall into the trap of only writing white characters, which is completely misrepresentative of our beautiful, vibrant world and connected humanity. I firmly believe this has to be done with care and diligence, because white authors can cause quite a bit of harm if they don't take the proper steps to write characters of other cultures. I'm by no means perfect, and I'm sure there are still several mistakes in this manuscript which are inadvertent and unintended, but I was dedicated to making sure I did my best to write Cyrus's character with care.

Thanks so much to fellow author Harper Miller, who did the sensitivity read for this book. The feedback was clear and extremely eye-opening. And, yes, it was very uncomfortable to read. It's hard to take feedback on your own work, and on your own biases. But Harper's feedback and suggestions were fantastic and I did my best to implement them, which made this novel so much better. I'm so appreciative of the time and care she took to help me improve. Harper also writes steamy love stories with awesome characters and I urge you to check out her books here: https://www.authorharpermiller.com/.

On another note, I want to address the use of Percocet in this novel. I, like probably many of you, lost a very close friend to the opioid epidemic a few years ago. She was young and had her whole life ahead of her, and it was devastating. For those who've also lost someone, know that I don't take the mention of this drug lightly. Instead, I thought it a good way to show how doctors—even well-meaning and altruistic doctors like Doc Viv—can be manipulated into using a drug by pharmaceutical companies. I worked in medical sales for years and saw the dark underside of Corporate America's involvement in medicine. While there are some wonderful companies, there are also some devious ones. The wide adoption of prescribing opioids in the early 2000s is a good reminder how easily we can fall into the trap of just assuming something is safe. I thought of my friend, Maggie, as I wrote this book and send my love to her and her family, and to anyone you may have lost from this terrible epidemic we now find ourselves in.

On a happier note, boy, I sure have surrounded myself with some awesome people. You have to if you want to be successful, and this team makes me so much better. Thanks to Megan McKeever, who is my editor, unofficial therapist, 3am random email recipient, and so much more! I have no idea if her other authors drive her as crazy as I do, but I'm extremely thankful for her help and guidance. Thanks to Bryony Leah, my amazing proofreader, across-the-pond grammar savior, fellow Jo Bros lover and overall lovely person. And thanks to Anthony O'Brien, who somehow manages to splice together the random images I send him into fantastic covers. He has a gift and I'm so glad I found him!

Thanks to fellow science geek, romance lover and blogger extraordinaire, Bonnie Natola (@bonsiesbooks). This woman is a firecracker and I'm so lucky to have connected with her, and to call her a friend! And thanks to all of the amazing ARC readers I reached out to who were open to reading and reviewing this and other books of mine. I'm so very thankful for you!

And, lastly, thanks to all my friends and family who read these books (and who leave reviews!). I appreciate you more than you know.

Okay, I have to go write more books. See you in A Timeline Restored! (Hint: Alora and Eli = HOT ... and Elle and Zach = the cutest damn things you've ever seen! Happy reading!)

About the Author

USA Today bestselling author Rebecca Hefner grew up in Western NC and now calls the Hudson River of NYC home. In her youth, she would sneak into her mother's bedroom and read the romance novels stashed on the bookshelf, cementing her love of HEAs. A huge Buffy and Star Wars fan, she loves an epic fantasy and a surprise twist (Luke, he IS your father).

Before becoming an author, Rebecca had a successful twelve-year medical device sales career. After launching her own indie publishing company, she is now a full-time author who loves writing strong, complex characters who find their HEAs.

Rebecca can usually be found making dorky and/or embarrassing posts on TikTok and Instagram. Please join her so you can laugh along with her!

Follow Rebecca Here:

www.rebeccahefner.com